THE CRACKS
IN OUR ARMOR

Anna Gavalda

THE CRACKS
IN OUR ARMOR

*Translated from the French
by Alison Anderson*

Europa
editions

Europa Editions
214 West 29th Street
New York, N.Y. 10001
www.europaeditions.com
info@europaeditions.com

Copyright © Le Dilettante, 2017
First Publication 2019 by Europa Editions

Translation by Alison Anderson
Original title: *Fendre l'armure*
Translation copyright © 2019 by Europa Editions

Library of Congress Cataloging in Publication Data is available
ISBN 978-1-60945-496-8

Gavalda, Anna
The Cracks in Our Armor

Book design by Emanuele Ragnisco
www.mekkanografici.com

Cover illustration by Mariachiara Di Giorgio

Prepress by Grafica Punto Print – Rome

Printed in the USA

CONTENTS

For Bénédicte

THE CRACKS
IN OUR ARMOR

Courtly Love

1

I said stop. Don't push it."

I didn't feel like going at all. I was exhausted, I felt ugly and, worse still, I hadn't shaved. Times like this I'm completely useless, and since I know nothing will come of it I always end up as smashed as a bomb site.

I know, I'm too sensitive but hey, I can't help it. If I'm not looking my best, with my pussy all neat and tidy, I can't just leave myself open for anything.

Never mind the fact I got in an argument with my dumbass boss while I was finishing my cages, and that really sapped my energy.

It was all over that new ProCanina line, *Puppy Sensitive.*

"I won't sell it," I said to him, over and over, "I won't sell it. It's complete bullshit. *Enhances cerebral and visual development,*" I read, shoving his bag of kibble back at him, twenty-seven euros for a six-pound bag, *enhances cerebral development,* tell me another one. Hey, if that were true, they should eat it themselves, assholes.

My boss walked off, yelling about his report, and my behavior, and my language, and how I'll never get that permanent contract, yadda yadda yadda, but what the fuck do I care. He can't fire me and he knows it as well as I do. Since I've been working there, profits have doubled and I brought all my former clientele from Favrot as a dowry, so . . .

Up yours, time clock, up yours.

I don't know why he's so antsy when it comes to that supplier. I suppose the rep has been promising him all sorts of things. Smartphone cases shaped like kibble, toothpaste for his poodle, weekends by the seaside . . . Or hey, even better, a weekend by the seaside masquerading as a sales seminar so he can go get his rocks off, away from his old lady.

That would be just his style.

I was over at my friend Samia's. I was eating her mom's pastries and watching her straighten her hair, strand by strand by strand. It took forever. Like, wearing the veil, in comparison, is women's lib. I sat there licking my fingers—dripping with honey—and admiring her patience.

"But, uh . . . since when you sell stuff for pappies?" she asked.

"Huh?"

"That kibble, you said. *Pappy Sensitive.*"

"Nah. It's puppy. *Puh-peez.*" Samia's English is not great.

"Oh, sorry," she laughed, "so what's the problem? You don't like the way it tastes?"

I stared at her.

"Hey, take it easy," she went. "Don't look at me like that. What, I can't say anything anymore? And why don't you come with me tonight? Go on, *puh-leez* . . . C'mon, girl . . . For once, don't let me down."

"Whose party is it?"

"My brother's old roommate."

"I don't even know him."

"I don't either, but who cares! We go check it out, take our pick, go eenie-meenie, then talk about it!"

"Knowing your brother, it's gonna be another one of those bougie things."

"And so what? What's wrong with bougie? The food's yummy,

honey! They don't have to call everyone they know just to have decent stuff and in the morning you might even get fresh croissants."

I really wasn't in the mood. I wasn't about to tell her but I had a whole stack of episodes of *Sexy Nicky* to catch up on and I was really fed up with all her crap plans for lonely hearts.

The thought of taking the RER depressed me, I was cold and hungry, I smelled like bunny shit, and all I wanted was to be in bed, alone, with my series.

She put down her hair straightener thingie and knelt before me, rounding her lips into a heart, pressing her palms together.

Okay.

I walked over to her closet with a sigh.

Friendship.

The only thing that contributes to my cerebral development.

"Take my Jennyfer top!" she shouted from the bathroom, "It'll look great on you!"

"Uh, this really slutty thing?"

"What d'you mean, it's really pretty. And there's a little sequined animal on the front. It was made for you, honestly!"

Yeah sure.

I borrowed her pussy mower, took a shower, and practically dislocated my shoulders to get Messrs. Roro and Ploplo into her size XXS T-shirt with Glitter Kitty on the front.

Downstairs, by the mailboxes, I stopped and turned around to look at myself in the mirror, just to make sure you could see my Mushu's little beard sticking up above my low-rise jeans.

Nah, you couldn't, drat . . . I had to give a little downward tug on the waistline.

I love this tattoo. It's Mushu (the dragon in Mulan) (no seriously I love that cartoon, I've seen it at least a hundred and fifty-six times, and cried every time. Especially during the training when she manages to climb to the top of the pole.).

The guy who did the tattoo swore it was a real one, Ming dynasty and all, and I believe him, since he's Chinese, too.

"Wow. You rock."

Since she was my best friend, I didn't really catch her compliment, but when I saw the expression on the face of the guy coming out of the elevator I realized that, yeah, it worked.

He was helpless.

Sami pointed at the wall:

"Hey, M'sieu . . . There's a fire extinguisher over there . . . "

By the time it registered we were already running down the street toward the station, laughing and squeezing each other's hand tight because with those heels we were wearing we might as well have been Thumper and Bambi in *Holiday on Ice*.

We took the 7:42 P.M. SCOP and we checked to make sure—in case the party got dicey—that there was a ZEUS bus to get us back at four minutes to one A.M. Then Samia got out her sudokus so she'd look like some rocking bluestocking otherwise they pester you on public transport, I swear, nonstop.

2

Bougie sort of place, tell me about it. There were at least four coded electronic doors to go through before we could start digging into the potato chips.

Four!

I swear, the police station in Bobigny is like a Playmobil farm in comparison.

At one point I even thought we'd be spending the night by the recycling bin. I was going crazy. This was Sami all over, what a drag, of the sort my-credit-card-is-maxed-out-but-I'll-use-it-anyway.

Luckily some guy came out to take his toy Schnauzer for a wee, otherwise we'd be there still.

We rushed over to him. I think the poor guy freaked out. Even though I'd never hurt an animal. Even if Schnauzies, gotta confess, they're not really my thing. I've never liked wire-hairs. The beard, whiskers, hair on their bellies, around their paws and all that, honestly it's just way too much maintenance.

We made such a fuss on all the entry phones that eventually someone let us in and once we were out of the cold we headed straight for the antifreeze.

While I was sipping a lukewarm, borderline nauseating glass of punch I did a 360 degree reconnoiter of the room to evaluate the merchandise on offer.

Meh. I was already missing my series. Nothing but milk-fed little mama's boys. Not my drug of preference *at all*.

*

If I understood correctly, it was some sort of artists' do. Photo exhibition of some woman who'd been to India or somewhere. I didn't really look too closely. Since I was actually in Paris and not in the banlieue for once, I didn't want people to go showing me more poverty.

I had all I needed at home.

Sami was already alarming some sort of Goth with a flyaway lock of hair and his mom's Maybelline kohl and honestly I couldn't tell what her freak-show intentions were until I noticed that her little stud-bejeweled Dracula had a buddy in Gucci right there next to him.

And then: okay. Then it clicked. This would make for a perfect selfie.

Because I know her, my little Sami. The thought that for the first time in her life she might be rubbing hips with a Gucci belt that wasn't of the flea market variety, that already cleared the way for the guy.

Or for his prick, shall we say.

So I wouldn't be a third wheel, I went on a tour of the apartment.

Big deal.

Nothing but books.

I felt sorry for the cleaning lady.

I leaned down to look at a photograph of a cat. It was a Birman. You could tell from the little white socks. I like them, but they have a delicate constitution. And then there's the price tag . . . You can get two Siamese for one Birman, pretty pricey paws. And it reminded me that I still have all the scratching posts and rope trees to unpack. Whew. I hardly have any room left on the shelves. I'll wait until the sale on the—

"Allow me to introduce Arsène."
Fuck, he really gave me a fright, stupid jerk.

I hadn't noticed him. The guy in the armchair right behind me. He was hiding in the shadows and all you could see was his leg. I mean, his effeminate sock and black ankle boot. And his hand on the armrest. His big hand, playing with a tiny box of matches.

"My cat. My father's, to be exact. And Arsène, allow me to introduce . . . "
"Uh . . . Lulu."
"Lulu?"
"Yes."
"Lulu . . . Lulu . . . " he repeated, adopting a super mysterious tone of voice, "Lulu, that could be Luce or Lucie. Or Lucille . . . Even Ludivine . . . Unless it's . . . Lucienne?"
"Ludmila."
"Ludmila! How lucky! A heroine straight out of Pushkin! And what about your Ruslan, my dear? Still out looking for you with that rascal Rogday?"

Help.
Fuck. Whenever there's one that escapes from the center for the disabled, you can be sure he's got a tag with my name on it.
Damn right. How lucky.

"Sorry?" I said.
He stood up and I saw his build was nothing like his feet. That he was even downright cute. Shoot, that really wasn't going to work for me.
He asked me if I wanted something to drink and when he came back with two glasses that weren't plastic cups but real

glass glasses from his kitchen, we went out on the balcony for a smoke.

I asked him whether Arsène was named after Arsène Lupin and his white gloves so that he'd get right away that I wasn't as dumb as I looked and that's when I saw a flicker of disappointment in his gaze. He congratulated me, in a kind of heavy-handed way, but you could tell he was thinking, Shit, she's not going to be as easy a lay as she looks, the bitch.

Yup. Don't judge a book, etc. I'm vulgar, but that's my camouflage. Like geckos on tree trunks or Arctic foxes whose coats change in winter, what you see does not reflect my true colors.

There are these hens, I can't remember what they're called, that have feathers behind their claws, that way they can erase their tracks as they move along—well I'm the same except it's the other way around, I cover my trail before I even come into contact with anyone.

And why? Because this body of mine distorts my nature.

(Even more so when I wear my friend Samia's flypaper T-shirts, I must confess.)

So we started with his cat then cats in general and then dogs and blah and blah how they're not as noble but way more affectionate and from there, no getting away from it, we came to my job.

He thought it was terrific when he found out I was the one in charge of all those critters over at the Animaland in Bel-Ébois.

"All of them?!"

"Yeah . . . Fishing worms, dogs, guinea pigs, gerbils, carp, parakeets, canaries, hamsters and, uh . . . rabbits—dwarf rabbits, lop rabbits, angoras . . . Then all the ones I can't remember because of the rum, but they're there, all right."

(To be honest I'm not the one in charge, but since he lived across from Notre-Dame and I live behind the Stade de France, I felt duty-bound to even out the playing field, so to speak.)

"That's magnificent."
"What is?"
"No, what I mean is, mesmerizing. Quite romantic."

Really? I thought. Lugging stuff around, labeling, lifting, piling bags of feed almost as heavy as you are, putting up with the customers—the fucking know-it-all breeders, the dog handlers who piss you off with their rates, the little old ladies who go on for hours with their tales of old abandoned kitties and then the folks who ask if you'll exchange their kid's dead hamster while they give a sigh, super pissed-off as if the hamster had been the wrong size. Dealing with bosses, seeing your schedule change because of some brown noser, fighting to go on your break, feeding the entire menagerie, checking the water dishes, keeping the dominant males apart, speeding the dying ones to a merciful death, disposing of the corpses, and changing over seventy litter boxes a day, you really think it's mesmer-thingy?

He must have, since he asked me a zillion questions.

And what about exotic pets, was it true that people kept pythons and cobras in their one-bedroom apartments, and did those mint snackies for dogs really work because his grandfather's lab had foul breath (after that he never said "my grandfather" when he referred to him, he always said "my Bon-Papa" as if it were some sort of Bonne Maman jam for rich people, really cute) and did I like rats, and was it true that the movie *Ratatouille* had started some sort of rat-mania, and had I ever been bitten, and was I vaccinated against rabies, and had

I ever picked up a snake, and which breeds were the most pop-
ular, and . . .

And what happened when they didn't get sold?

What did we do with puppies who'd outgrown their sell-by
date?

Did we kill them?

What about mice? Did we give them to labs when we had
too many?

And was it true that people flushed their turtles down the
toilet, that punks with dogs were real softies, that rabbits
didn't like cannabis plants, that there were crocodiles at large
in the Paris sewers and . . . and . . .

And I felt tipsy. In a good way. Not grumpy, just light-headed.

Pickled, in other words.

And because I love my job, frankly I didn't mind putting
my smock back on. Even in some swanky apartment and long
after closing time.

I told him about every aisle, from the shavings to the ceiling
and he was listening real attentively and saying, Brilliant.
Brilliant.

Brilliant.

"And fish, too?"

"Fish, too," I nodded.

"Go on. Tell me about them."

It was weird. I was having a really good time even though I
wasn't completely wasted.

It was . . . What was that word of his?

Mesmerizing.

"Well, Monsieur, first of all you have to choose between fresh
and salt water, because it won't be the same equipment. But
otherwise, if you want a decent aquarium, I would recommend

the very attractive angelfish, which swims majestically with its long, elegant fins, and then there's the discus, which is shaped like a disc and is truly magnificent . . . Then there are danios, brill, harlequin rasboras, and neon tetras, which are like jewels, with their fluorescent scales . . . Like glowworms, only in the water . . . And let's not forget the otocinclus, which are regular cleaners, the way they eat seaweed, and the hypostomus, which clean the windows as well and, uh, personally I really like the Indian loaches, with those triple black stripes on their body, very classy, but they tend to stay hidden at the bottom. You don't see them often. Then there are guppies . . . and gouramis, too. But you have to watch out for them, they're troublemakers. They like to eat the neons, that's the problem. Anyway, I'd advise you to get them very young, and raise them all together. And of course we have a wide range of aquariums. Aqualantis, Nano, Eheim, Superfish, and all the accessories available on the market, as well as a prime selection of exclusive imports. Gravel, pebbles, seaweed, plants, decors, filtration systems, water heaters, air pumps, and pH kits. So you see . . . it's all here."

This was the first time I'd ever met someone who was that interested, fascinated even, in my humdrum everyday routine.

The stockroom all the way at the far end of the store, the miles I have to walk, my fatigue, the constant concern about hygiene, the hassle dealing with mange, ringworm, feline influenza, and all the rest. Moreover, I think he was sincere. He really was interested. Otherwise we would have realized earlier on that we were freezing out there while I jabbered away, leaning on our elbows as we looked out at a wintry Paris.

I won't say he wasn't checking me out a little, snooping, but it was, uh, just the way he was: mellow. And this too was completely foreign to me. My boobs and me, we weren't used to all these fine manners.

When I began to get goose bumps he said we better go inside so we went back into the music and the smoke.

He hadn't finished closing the French doors when this super thin chick zeroed in on him asking him all frantic in a whiny voice where had he been, what was he doing, why was the music so rotten . . . and then she broke off because she had just added me to the equation.

That sobered her up real quick, the bitch.

"Oh, sorry," she simpered, "I didn't know you were in such, uh, *fine* company . . . "

(Oh yes. I didn't dream it. She went real heavy on the word "fine," little slut.)

And he answered, with a catlike smile:

"No. You didn't know."

She looked at me, pulling as hard as she could on the corners of her big mouth to send me a nice smile that said, more or less, "The hormones have already been squirted and the territory marked, fatso, so get the hell out like right now otherwise I'll scratch your eyes out," and then she hooked her arm through his to drag him over to the others.

So I went looking for Sami, with no luck.

She was probably already en route to Italy, by way of the Bermuda Triangle . . .

Nothing left to eat, the music was crap, sort of loud but not so loud you disturb the neighbors, and all the guests had clumped into little groups, not letting anyone else in.

I took a sweater out of my bag and put it on so that my Mushu wouldn't get cold on the tip of his nose, and before I went to find my parka I scanned the apartment one last time just so I could say goodbye to the one person who'd spoken to me all evening.

Couldn't find him. This guy who'd been so passionate not two minutes ago had completely flaked on me the minute that tramp got her claws into him.

Bah . . . It happens. Well, to me, anyway. Often, even. The minute a guy shows an interest in something besides my merchandise that interest doesn't last very long, as a rule.

A quick score or out the door. My des-tin-y.

I know I've just been listing all the hassles I have at work but the thing is, not a single one of my animals would ever treat me that way. Never.

When I spend time on them, and treat them the way I should, and pay attention to their well-being, they don't forget it.

And no matter the time of day, whenever I go by their cages, they each have their own way of demonstrating their friendship.

They stop eating, and look up, some of them chirp, others squeak, others peep, or hop from one foot to the other, or whistle or sing, even, and as soon as I'm gone, hup, they start munching again.

And then, whenever there's one that leaves, I'm sad. Even if it's just a little white mouse or a dumb-ass parakeet, and even when the customers seem nice.

I feel all weird inside and I go all quiet, for hours.

Samia says it's because my parents are far away and I'm withholding, for want of love. I don't know. I think I'm just really stupid, is all.

Whoa. Fucking cold. Inside. Outside. In my head and in the street. My fingers felt like popsicles and my morale was no better.

Exactly the sort of time when it's a really bad idea to start soul-searching and exactly the sort of time when you just can't help it.

*

I was single. I lived in a crap studio. Even smaller than the lounge kennel at work. Every Sunday I went to see my sister and played with her kids so she could help her husband finish their house, and during vacations I never went anywhere because I'd be pet-sitting for my favorite customers and a few tenants in the building. And Shirley, too, the concierge's little Yorkie. It gave me a pretext not to go see my aunt and uncle and besides, it paid a whole month's rent.

And the rest of the time, I was at work.

Sometimes I went out with girlfriends and got myself involved in these plots, each one more hopeless than the next. Well, when I say "plots," that's not really the right word, but you get the picture.

I have a colleague who's been pestering me to look for love on the internet, but that is just not my thing.

Every time I've ordered something because I trusted the photo I've been disappointed in the result. People are mental with their computers. They really believe in what they see when all it is, is stuff for sale in a bright shopwindow.

No one ever imagines I'm like this. That I'm the sort who sits there all alone taking stock in my head, that I know how to tell good words from bad and I even have opinions about the internet.

Anyway, what does anybody know, so . . .

Like me, for example, a few hours ago I didn't even know there were two islands smack in the middle of Paris. I only just realized, standing there chatting on that balcony. At the age of twenty-three, that's pathetic.

I was running like crazy toward Châtelet—I was afraid of

missing my RER and I really didn't have the means to take a taxi just then—when I heard:

"Princess! Princess! Not so fast! You're going to lose your slipper!"

No way.

I could not believe it.

There was Special Agent Mulder again . . .

Maybe there was one last thing he wanted to ask me? The price of a canary or a ferret exercise ball?

He was bent double trying to catch his breath:

"Wha . . . Why did you leave . . . so . . . so soon? Do you . . . fff . . . do you want to go for . . . fff . . . a nightcap?"

I told him I didn't want to miss the ZEUS, which made him laugh, and then he offered to see me back to Olympus and that made me sad.

I was in over my head and I knew I wouldn't be able to stay in the game for long. That I'd have to sleep with him if I wanted to go on playing. Yes, I knew it, that apart from my menagerie I didn't have a lot in stock and as for my other assets, they were way more common.

So I didn't say anything.

We hurried down the stairs together and since he didn't have a ticket I motioned to him to squeeze up close next to me to go through the turnstiles.

Ha, ha. I too got my Garfield smile.

The station was deserted and the atmosphere was creepy: a dealer who'd set up a quick-stop shop at the entrance to the tunnel, a few partygoers, already pretty wasted, and some cleaning workers on their way home, dead tired.

We sat on the last free bench all the way at the end of the platform and waited.

Old silence.

He didn't talk, didn't ask any more questions, and I was too scared it would show—my wasted years at school, how I failed my diploma—so I played the gecko: I sat there motionless and blended into my surroundings.

I read the billboards, looked at my feet and the scraps of newspaper on the ground, I tried to guess the missing words and wondered if he was really going to follow me all the way home. I was totally freaking out. I was ready to go clear out to Eurodisney by way of Orly to keep him from getting the slightest idea about my life and where I lived.

He was looking at people and you could tell he was dying to ask them as many questions as he'd asked me.

How much for a gram? Where's it from? What's your margin? And if all hell breaks loose, what do you do? You run into the tunnel, is that it? What about you? What sort of party was it? Birthday? Soccer match? Where are you headed now? And tell me, is your mom going to clean up all that puke, yet again? And you, Madam? Offices or a store? Is it hard work? Do they provide you with powerful vacuum cleaners at least? Where are you from? And why did you have to leave? How much did you have to pay the smugglers? Do you miss it? Yes? No? A little? And do you have children? Who is looking after them while you are waiting for your RER and it's past midnight, so far away from Mali?

After a while, to act the part and reestablish contact, off I go: "Looks like you're interested in people."

"Yes," he murmured, "that's true. In everybody . . . Really everybody . . . "

"Do you work for the police?"

"No."

"What do you do?"

"I'm a poet."

Fuck did I feel stupid. I didn't even know it was still a profession.

He must have realized, because he turned to face me and said: "You don't believe me?"

"Yes, yes, I do, but, uh . . . it's not really a job, is it."

"Really?"

And all of a sudden, just like that, he turned really sad. His face gray, his eyes like an abandoned cocker spaniel's. Seriously, this wasn't much fun anymore and I couldn't wait for my pumpkin to show up.

"Maybe you're right," he said, in a low voice, "maybe it isn't a profession. But then what is it? An illusion, a favor, an honor? An imposture? An inevitability? Or a convenient affectation in order to chat up a pretty girl in a sinister place while waiting for the god of thunder?"

Fuck me. Back into the fourth dimension.

This is what happens when you punch above your weight (in the human relations department), you lose your balance with the first puff of air.

And that lazy stupid useless RER still not showing up . . .

After a silence that was even heavier than before, given the fact he wasn't looking around him anymore now but inside him and what he was finding was way less "mesmerizing" or "romantic" than two druggies, three drunks, and one worn-out cleaning lady, he said, never looking up from his thoughts:

"And yet. You, Ludmila, for example. You. You are the proof that poets have a reason to be on this earth. You are . . . "

I didn't react, not a millimeter, because I was dead curious to find out what I was.

"A dream of a blason."

"A *what?*"

A flash of light. Now he was back among us.

"In the sixteenth century," he began, waffling again, all happy and sure of himself, "all the rhymers and rhymesters and versifiers and other dreamers went about it, more specifically, they composed paeans to those divine charms you occasionally favor us with. To produce a blason was to magnify, as simply and delicately as possible, the various parts of the female body and you, lovely Loulia, you, when I . . . "

He moved closer to touch my head, and said softly:
"Long, lovely, locks unbound
All the better my heart to bind . . . "
Then his hand lingered on my piercings and rings:
"Oh ear impressing upon the heart
What the lips express.
Oh ear into which one must speak
As it tends gracefully toward the cheek . . . "
which made me squint:
"Brow that chases and taunts the clouds
In keeping with its noble arch . . . "
Then, like in some kid's nursery rhyme, his index finger went gently nudging along my face:
"Pretty little nose, polished and well-fashioned
Neither short nor long, most well-proportioned . . . "
I was smiling. Then he tapped on my teeth:
"Oh, lovely teeth, thus joined and well united
What pleasure brings this fetching sight!
How drear when there is naught to bite!"
So, there, I burst out laughing.

And as I was laughing, I knew my goose was cooked. Or anyway that it could be. All of a sudden there was the smell of something burning.

"The train is approaching the station," blinked the sign. I stood up.

He followed me.

We were the only people around and we sat down facing each other.

And once again this weird old silence lost in the sound of the wheels on the rails. After a few minutes had gone by, he added, as if nothing had happened:

"Of course, there are many others . . . Blasons, that is. You can imagine that between your hair and the tips of your toes there are, well, *there could be*, so many other sources of inspiration . . . "

"Oh, yeah?" I said, holding back my smile.

"The most famous one, for example. *The Blason of the Beautiful Nipple*, by the great Clément Marot."

"I get it . . . "

I was forcing myself to count the lamps in the tunnel to keep a straight face.

"Or the navel, for example. That *Little Knot which, from divine hands, after all else was perfect, was the very last event,*" he looked at me with a smile, *"that little corner whence moved desire for tickling delight . . . "*

"Belly button, too, huh?" I said, sounding astonished, like some little brown noser who's way too interested in the teacher's bullshit.

"Indeed. As I said . . . The navel, and its neighbors a bit further down . . . "

What a night. What a Martian pickup act. Complete and utter BS. If someone had told me one day that I'd be on the D-line at midnight with Victor Hugo himself and that, on top of it, it would give me this warm feeling in my belly, frankly I'd look around to see who they were talking about.

So I said, coy as could be:

"So? Don't you remember those ones?"

"I do, but . . . uh . . . "

"Uh, what?"

"Well, I don't want to shock anyone. We're in a public place, after all," he whispered, shifting his eyes to indicate the completely deserted car.

And then, at that point in my life, just before we pulled into the Gare du Nord, I told myself three things:

One: I want to sleep with this sweet duck. I want to because I've been having fun with him and if you think about it there is nothing nicer on earth than having fun in bed with a sweet boy.

Two: I am going to pay for it. Again. This is the sort of thing that's doomed from the get-go. A sort of war of the worlds, culture clash, class struggle and all the rest. So I won't give, anything. I'll get undressed, I'll look after that part of me that's hungry, I'll have a great time, then I'll get the hell out. No swapping phone numbers, no text messages the morning after, no little kisses on the neck, no cuddles, no smiles, no nothing.

Nothing tender. Nothing that might leave a memory. This blason thingy, okay, but I act super blasé, otherwise on Monday morning I'll start crying again like a stupid cow the minute I reach for my baby bunnies.

Because that swarm of tactile little poems may have been fine and dandy but it was typical of a really well-oiled pickup stunt. To know all those poems by heart he must have done this a million times already.

Besides, I don't even have long hair.

So silence up there while we get this straight, before the attack. The road map is really simple:

Good evening sir, Welcome, sir, Goodbye, sir.

See you again sometime.

Three: Not at my place. Not there.

"What are you thinking about?" he said, worriedly.
"A hotel room."
"Oh, Lord," he moaned, as if he were really shocked, "these Pushkin heroines . . . I should have known."
A poet in a good mood is really gorgeous.
I laughed.
"Oh laughter, welcome me into your heavenly realm . . ."

What better way to put it.

A fter what came next, after the little muff secreted by vermillion stud or ruby buckle, and the round little derrière, so sweet and impregnable, embedded twixt two hills where no enemy dare approach, after all these hours of good things and banter in Old French from a bygone era, while we were recovering and he was holding me to his chest, I asked him:

"And what about you?"

"Sorry?"

"All of this is stuff you've read in books, but could you make me one just like that, on the spot? For me and me alone?"

"What do you mean, a baby?" he said, pretending to be horrified.

"No, dummy. A poem."

He was silent for so long that I thought he'd fallen asleep, and I was about to do the same myself when he took a lock of my hair in his fingers.

While I wriggled my Mushu's little wings on my buttocks, he whispered in my ear:

"Little Saint George of an evening,
And this my only glory,
Employing naught but jargon
Did I then slay this dragon."

I smiled in the dark and then I waited until it was time.

I didn't want to sleep. That would have been too trusting, too much letting go.

For sure I was already hurting in spite of myself; for sure. When people make you laugh, however much your heart may pretend otherwise, it is already fucked.

4

I n the end, I took the 6:06 IVON.
   I was with more or less the same people as at Châtelet a few hours earlier except for the cleaning crew: they were new.

Everyone was half-comatose.

My forehead against the cold glass windowpane, I chewed on an imaginary piece of gum to keep my throat from choking me.

I really felt like crying. I clung to stupid things. Fatigue, cold, the night . . . I kept thinking: It's because you didn't get enough sleep, but later on, after a good shower, you'll see, you'll feel better. And I turned the volume up as high as it would go to drown everything out again.

Adele in my earbuds. I loved her voice. It was my voice. Always on the verge of breaking. So of course I didn't even make it to the end of the song.

Anyway at least like that my eye makeup was already removed.

Screw, lay, get laid, stuff, shag, bang, get it on, hump, do the business, not to mention the ubiquitous f-word . . . All these substitutes we use for make love when we know damn well there's no love and there never will be. But I—and I've never told anyone, especially not Samia—when I . . . I always feel it.

My body is . . . My body is who I am. It is me, too. It's *me* who's there living inside it and . . .

And that is why, every time, I get fleeced.

Or maybe tarred and feathered, I should say.

Every time.

I have never betrayed anyone.

Ever.

I've always shared.

Oh, look. There they are again, the high-rises, the tags, the police stations, the hoodies, and the spit.

And here we are, home again, jiggety-jig.

When I left the IVON (that guy, the poet, I never even found out his name), I took a deep breath and headed straight for my comforter.

I blew on my fingers, smiled to myself, gave myself a pep talk. Come on, I said, come on . . . This time, it was different, you got blasoned.

After all.

How classy is that?

Resistance Fighter

1

I'd moved with the kids into a tiny apartment behind the Panthéon.

Fifth floor no elevator, run-down, funky, everything lopsided, I was subletting from my former thesis advisor's sister, a woman I'd never met in person, and I'd been unable to tell her over the phone just how long I intended to stay. Temporary solution, temporary situation, temporary arrangement, those were her words and I was careful not to contradict her. Of course. Of course. Everything was temporary. I got it.

Through the dormer in my study I could see the emergency exit from the Great Men's sanctuary and I liked that little door. I liked the thought of working, sleeping, cooking, clenching my teeth, raising my children, and starting all over again in the shadow of the ghosts of Alexandre Dumas, Voltaire, Victor Hugo, and Pierre and Marie Curie. It's ridiculous, I know, but I swear that's how I felt. I really believed in the thought that those people were helping me. I'd had to cram most of our former life into storage, and we weren't allowed to put our name on the letterbox. A detail, but the devil's in the details and in my case he could be really pleased with himself because even though I did have my mail addressed to an uncle, living here without a letterbox, so high up, in such shabby accommodation, and with for sole support the bones that were more alive than we were, we weren't really here anymore. Neither here nor anywhere and, since we weren't really here anymore we—Raphaël, five, Alice, three and a half, and me, thirty-four at the time—insidiously cut ourselves off from the rest of the world.

Their father had died in a car crash the previous year. A depressive, elegant, conscientious man who left me not knowing what to think as to the accidental nature of his collision with a shrine, by the side of a deserted road in the Finistère, but perfectly enlightened regarding our material situation since, in addition to two orphans and one very damaged Jaguar, he had left me the "death benefit" of a life insurance policy that would keep us going for a few more years. How many, I had no idea.

He was much older than me, he knew he was sick, he couldn't stand the thought of imposing his decline on us, and he was constantly telling me I ought to find a younger, healthier lover, that I had to do it for my own sake and for the children's, to put his soul to rest. *Above all to put my soul to rest, my love . . . You know how selfish I am . . .* I kept a muzzle on him for as long as I could, by dint of kisses, protests, denials, acts of bravado, laughter, and tears, but in the end, he outwitted me all the same.

I was angry with him. For a long time it seemed to me that far from sparing us his decline, he had imposed it on us forever. I didn't invite his children to the funeral, or even his parents, I went alone with him to the crematorium at Père-Lachaise and when I took the métro back the other way I was hiding a still-warm urn under my sweater. That same evening I got completely wasted with Lorenz W., his associate, and I begged him to fuck me. I was feeling very sentimental at the time, but young widows are often very sentimental. I lived with my head stuck in a shrine for a few months and then I decided to move, and this little apartment came to the rescue.

No furniture, no memories, no neighbors, no butcher, no baker, no newspaper vendor, no café waiter, no wine merchant, no dry cleaners' employee who'd known him and grown very fond of him because he was a delightfully endearing man, no little classmates who were as hurtful as they were ingenuous, no sympathetic schoolteachers far too sweet to be sincere, no points of reference, no routine, no letterbox, no doorbell, no elevator, no safety net, no nothing: at last we were able to ease up on the sorrow.

Our life now fit in a space hardly bigger than a pocket handkerchief, its four corners unfolding as follows: the mini-market downstairs, the nursery school on the rue Cujas, the paths through the Luxembourg Gardens, and, last but not least, the Bombardier pub which huddled just across from the Saint-Étienne-du-Mont church. Every afternoon, we stopped in that square after school and Raphaël and Alice drank their lemon sodas while tallying their bruises, their marbles, their Pokémon cards, the stars in their notebooks, and who knows what else, while their *maman* slowly but surely got hammered.

Once the children were in bed, I often went back down onto the pavement outside the Bombardier just to mingle silently, pint in hand, with the clusters of students from the Latin Quarter.

Yes, that's what I did. Yes, I locked my little ones in at night and left them to their fate. Did they have nightmares? Were they afraid? Did they ever wake up? Did they ever call out for me?
I don't think so.
Children are so wise . . .

The moment my love first imagined his shrine, he started drinking, and I often went with him. I was along for the ride, after all, and when he was no longer there I just kept on going without him. I had a drinking problem, I won't deny it. Oh but yes, look, I am still denying it. I didn't have an alcohol problem, I was an alcoholic. (It's awful, rereading this and cringing at that last word, stumbling over it, more like, wondering if I wasn't exaggerating a little and was I still the sentimental young widow I mentioned above, so I went to check the definition of the word *alcoholic* in a dictionary: *A person who drinks too much alcohol*.) Right. I drank too much alcohol. I didn't want to elaborate on the subject, those who know, know, and don't need anyone to tell them how ingeniously the brain will help you bend your elbow, and those who don't know cannot understand. There comes a time when you realize that alcohol (and all the thoughts that go with it—struggle, resist, haggle, give in, deny, gain ground, fight, negotiate, exult, surrender, blame, advance, retreat, stumble, fall, lose) has become the most important activity of the day. Excuse me. The only activity of the day. Those who have ever tried to stop smoking —be it once or several times, but always in vain—will have a sense of how psychologically wretched this inane relationship with oneself has turned out to be. The only difference—and what a difference—is that other people do not view smoking as shameful. That's it. Let's change the subject.

I would rouse the children from their beds, get them dressed, butter their toast, pour their hot chocolate, take them to school, drink a coffee on the rue Soufflot while leafing through the newspaper, do some shopping, tidy our little home, get their lunch ready, go back to get them on the rue Cujas, feed them, take Raphaël back to class, come straight home with Alice fast as I could so she wouldn't fall asleep in her stroller, put her down for her nap, read detective stories that I had bought for fifty centimes or a euro from the boxes outside Gibert Jeune, Boulinier, or the bouquinistes on the banks of the Seine, wake her up, bring her along when I picked up her brother at school (little girl rested and babbling, big brother free at last and grinning, best time of day), take them to the Luxembourg gardens, watch them play, then home for their shower, and dinner, and I would read them stories, tuck them in, and kiss them goodnight.

And all that time, the vise of alcohol never loosened.

Never, and with varying degrees of assertiveness, depending on whether the moon was in my belly, sapping my energy, or whether my love had come to whisper in my ear without warning. When he was just passing by to make sure everything was all right, then I was fine, but when he too would weigh upon my belly, coming back at night and demanding his share of the bed, his share of life, his share of us, I would get back out of bed, in tears, and go downstairs and get bombed.

Our life, as I said, would fit in a handkerchief.

And then, one morning, I noticed you.

2

I noticed you because you were beautiful.

I was standing with my elbows on the counter, nursing my too-short nights as I read the day's news or eavesdropped on my neighbors' conversations by the sugar bowl, and I spotted you in the mirror above the bar. You always sat there, all the way at the back, in the same place.

I admired your style, your poise, your refinement, your hands. I liked your cheerfulness, your smiles, that way you had of being here and completely elsewhere, as if you had just left the embrace of a lover or were about to go and meet them. You were sexy, and you looked as if you must be smart, too, you were perfect, and yet there was always something inexplicably untidy about you, too, a strand of hair, a collar askew, a crease, a watchband too loose, a worn-out handbag, a belt fastened wrong, a crease at your lips, shadows under your eyes, and this made you . . . I was going to write "irresistible," but that's too predictable. Irrevocable.

Yes, irrevocable. Ever since there has been a Paris, people have talked, written, fantasized about Parisian women, and when I looked at you I said to myself: there, that's it, she's it. She's *the* Parisian woman, and that's all there is to it.

I was all the more aware of your beauty in that the mirror also reflected my own dreary counterpart, and the moment I saw it, I returned to stirring my coffee. I looked like nothing, skinny, out of sorts, I'd been wearing the same two pairs of jeans for months, and my dead husband's shirts, my dead husband's cashmere sweaters, my dead husband's scarves and his jackets, too. I'd gotten my hair cut very short so I wouldn't have to bother with it, I'd stopped wearing makeup and perfume, I'd stopped jogging but I never wore anything but my running shoes, I had a cavity, maybe even two, and couldn't care less, I drank too much, I was dehydrated, my hands were rough, my skin was dry, my body was dry, and everything inside me had bad breath.

You have since confessed that you had been watching me, too, and that you envied my casual, classy look. What a joke.

You had noticed the elegant cotton patches on the pockets of my worn-out jeans, the soft quality of my overlong cardigans, the way the cuffs doubled as mittens and how I shrouded myself in fine tweed and other fabrics.

You thought it was chic, you said, so chic . . .

You always ordered a small café au lait and a tartine, and you scraped the excess butter off with your little spoon, and you spent most of the time on your phone texting. You leaned over the screen and smiled. It wasn't hard to figure out that you were in love, and you began your days chatting with a man (or a woman?) who made you happy. Sometimes your smiles were moist and your dimples more alluring. What do you call it when a person is smiling and sending sexy messages? That they have started their day by sexting? Yes, every morning you would bite into a chunk of fresh baguette dipped in café au lait while you brought someone you loved up to date on your life, that much was obvious.

And there were times when your phone stayed in your bag next to your cup, silent. You were every bit as pretty but you looked a little lost, disoriented. On those days you would look around, and I think that's when we would exchange a little smile of complicity. Nothing friendly, really, just courtesy between two regulars at the same watering hole. People often say that Parisians are hard, but they never mention these moments of complicity they share among themselves. So we were familiar faces, but we might never have said a word to each other had Raphaël's teacher not gotten sick, which meant one morning I came back to the Café de la Sorbonne with my two kids in tow.

We sat down at the table next to you, deliberately, I must admit, and we weren't even settled before you started gazing hungrily at my little daughter. Life had not yet taught Alice that she wasn't really a princess, and she responded to your eager gaze by turning on the charm, and I saw how you melted when she showed you her security blanket, and her brother's, her decal tattoo, and her brother's, her marbles, and her brother's, crossing and uncrossing her pudgy little legs all the while and constantly readjusting the tiny sequined barrette which was her crown.

Someone ought to write about it someday: the grace and elegance of very little girls.

The children monopolized your attention and we hardly spoke that day. I found out that your name was Mathilde because Raphaël asked you, but I didn't say anything. I kept quiet because I'd hardly slept, I kept quiet because I was going to have to go grocery shopping with the children under my feet and that annoyed me (you see, that's alcoholism: thanks to the luminous presence of two children you finally meet the woman who's had you dreaming for weeks, and these children, in addition to being exquisite, have the good taste of being your children, and all four of you are sharing an exorbitantly-priced breakfast in a café in a city that sets the whole world dreaming, and yet you can only think about one thing, worse yet, you are *obsessed* with one thought alone: under which item, size-wise, volume-wise, a cereal box for example, are you going to hide your bottle of Johnnie Walker, in the crap plastic basket at the pathetic little grocery store on the ground floor of your building?). I kept quiet because I had nothing to say, I kept quiet because it was deafening, the noise in my brain, I kept quiet because I wasn't used to speaking anymore, I kept quiet because I had lost.

On the days that followed you didn't come to the Café de la Sorbonne. Then there were the school holidays, I think it was the February break, and one morning, when I'd already gotten out of the habit of looking out for you, you came to lean up against the bar next to me. You said hello, you ordered an Americano, and we didn't speak. As I turned to one side to fish for some coins in my pocket, you put your hand on my forearm and said, "Leave it, my treat," and it was only then, at that moment, when I turned to face you to thank you, that I saw your face crumple. I put my hand on yours and you burst into tears. "Sorry," you said, laughing, apologizing, "sorry, sorry." I left my hand where it was and I stopped looking at you.

I don't know how long we stood there not moving, you entrusting me with your sorrow and me enfolding it with my own. At one point you murmured: "Your children . . . they're so sweet," and I broke down.

The proprietor came over, gently scolding us. "What's going on, ladies? What is it? Don't you like it here? You're going to scare all the customers away! What can I offer you to make you feel better—a shot of calvados?"

Man, did that make me happy.

We downed it in one gulp. You choked, I could breathe again, and under the liberating effect of a few ounces of helium in my veins, I invited you to come over for dinner that very evening.

You smiled, I asked you if you had something to write with, and on a coaster I copied out the address of my little abode. As well as, because of the downstairs buzzer, the name of those people who were not us.

3

Y ou showed up with your arms full: flowers, a cake, champagne, presents for the children . . . They were delighted.

Just delighted. Not because of the presents, but because you were there. This was the first time the outside world had ever invited itself into our home, the first time that someone had made the climb to come and see us; life returning.

You didn't know that at the time, and you thought it was the Corolle doll, the bow and arrow, the stickers, the magical baby bottle, and the colored crayons that got them so excited, but you may recall that once all these treasures had been unwrapped all they wanted to do was take you by the hand to show you their room, their toys, their world, the ladder to their bunk bed, which was still a novelty to them, their class photos, the picture of their daddy, and of Toby, their former nanny's dog, and all their charming clutter. What you had brought them in the way of happiness was not material, and you played the game so well.

And it was then, on seeing how moved you were, how curious and attentive, listening and learning by heart the names of all their stuffed animals, baby dolls, classmates, and Wigglytuffs and Jigglypuffs and Slowpokes and Psyducks and other Pokémon, each one more improbable than the next, that I understood you were dying for children the way I was dying of thirst.

We watched them eat their dinner, and then Alice insisted you help her into her nightie and undo her braids and brush her hair, at length, which you did, constantly remarking on how silky it was, how curly and blond, how nice it smelled . . . And you also read them a story, and then another, and then a third, until finally I stepped in to free you from the children and your distress.

It was while we were chatting, doing justice to a delicious risotto and your bottle of champagne, that you said how "chic" I was, and I rolled my eyes to the sky, to the ceiling, shall we say, the roof beams, and then we went into the living room, which meant we went to sit six feet further away.

(I'll open a parenthesis here because I think it is important to mention our living room. Yes, it seems to me that what comes next in this story is in some way connected to the wizardry of my sofa, and without it, we would not have become friends that evening. Later, maybe, later of course, later for sure, but not that evening. Because I know what I'm like: when I love it's for life, but I don't love easily. Especially not in that period of absolute lockdown, for reasons of absolute security. This was not the time to let anything seep into my hermetic self. Even love. Especially love. No way. I was sealed off, absolutely watertight.

(The apartment we lived in came furnished, with all the depressing details that implies—heavy plates, flimsy cutlery, sagging beds, synthetic curtains, ludicrous tchotchkes (there was, and the children remember it, too, a stuffed piranha on a pedestal above the fireplace), chairs that were too high, and one sofa, dead ugly. Bit by bit I replaced everything—the time I spent wandering down the aisles of department stores was time not drowned in the bottom of a glass—but for the beds and the sofa it took a courage I didn't have. I would have had to arrange for delivery, which meant fixing a date and planning something in the future, and that was out. It was too much to ask. But it just so happened that the week before your visit, the three of us went to the Marché Saint-Pierre to buy some fabric for the school carnival. Accommodate the future, no thanks, but dress up the present, doll it up, deny it, trick it by making costumes: with pleasure. Alice, would you believe, wanted a princess gown and we wallowed in clouds of tulle, gauze, chiffon, sateen, and Swiss muslin, whereas Raphaël, would you believe, wanted to dress up as a Pokémon. It was thanks to his lack of imagination that we came upon a tiny shop on the rue d'Orsel, a gold mine of fake fur. Mink, fox, weasel, chinchilla, rabbit, Pikachu, Chihuahua, we didn't know where to look or how to carry it all and I had to call a taxi to the rescue to help us home with this lode of caresses stuffed into huge plastic bags.

(That very evening I transformed our awful sofa into the belly of Oum-Popotte. This wasn't my brilliant idea, but Raphaël's. Or rather, Claude Ponti's, a marvelous children's author who is a genius at imagining the silkiest, cuddliest fur. Thus far I may have reveled a lot in my own sorrow, but I have not evoked my children's, and they had lost the funniest and kindest of daddies; in Ponti's books there always comes a moment where a little hero with a rough, hardscrabble life finds refuge in an embrace of infinite softness. It's impossible to describe. You have to read his books to understand what our new sofa meant to Alice and Raphaël. It could be the tummy of Oum-Popotte or of Oups' parents or of Foulbazar, or of little Pouf. It was no longer a sofa, it was a big, placid animal that enfolded them when they came home from school or felt forlorn, and it cocooned them in endless cuddles. And those cuddles were all the more tender in that I'd made some huge cushions so that they could hold that big beast in their arms, too. Dust mites be damned, those yards and yards of fur were far and away the wisest purchase of our entire convalescence.)

So, as I was saying, we moved into the living room, and you immediately flipped off your ballet flats to curl up against our faithful friend's midriff, folding your legs under you and surrounding yourself with cushions.

I was sitting in my favorite place, on the floor, in other words, and I watched as you surrendered to Oum-Popotte with the restful smile and cheerful face of a little girl who has had a very, very long day at school.

We looked at each other.

I offered you some herbal tea (alcoholics never drink) (and that is how you can identify them) and you asked me if I didn't have, rather, some stronger stuff on offer (oh, dear), no, but uh, oh, wait, we're in luck, I thought there might be a bottle of whisky here somewhere. What a godsend, really. I poured us each a good dose (since it was a furnished apartment I didn't have any smaller glasses), and with our chamomile firmly in hand we leaned back again, you against the furry spread, me against the wall.

We drank.

The children were asleep, we were lulled by the laughter and shouts of the revelers downstairs, the candles made it cozy, the music on the radio set the mood, and we looked at each other.

We knew nothing about one another apart from the fact that we were both of a nature to shed a few tears at a zinc bar on a winter morning in Paris.

We looked at each other, sized each other up, appraised each other.

You were sipping slowly and I tried to do the same. It was hard. I was down for the count, clinging to my glass as if it were the ropes around the ring. You leaned back, placed a cushion on your stomach and asked,

"Where is their father?"

Y ou listened and remained silent, I poured myself some more to drink and you knew, you didn't say anything, but I could tell that you could tell, the way I was quaffing my peaty dram, lapping it up, and then it was my turn to question you; your turn.

"What about you?" I said.

"What about me."

"Why are you here?"

Sidestep. Smile. Sigh.

"How long have you got?"

"All night," I replied, "all night."

5

Y ou looked down at your lap and murmured, "Well, I, uh . . . "
  I was watching you, I could tell it wasn't that you were trying to disentangle yourself from it but, rather, you were fingering each strand of thought in your mind, wondering which one would be solid enough to withstand once you started to pull on the whole ball of yarn.

We had all night, and I was used to staying up late, sitting there, flat out, with a glass in my hand. I was in no hurry. I watched you and still found you just as lovely and I wished my love were still there, to see you. I would have liked to introduce him to you. I would have like to introduce you to each other. He loved a pretty woman with a tender gaze and eyes full of mischief like yours. Of course he would have slipped out at some point but first he would have made us laugh. He liked more than anything to make clever women laugh. It was his way, he said, of making us human and of thanking us for existing and putting up with his presence among us. He got this silly gushing laughter out of us, the better to love us.

Thinking of him brought tears to my eyes and to see me sinking like that gave you the courage to take the plunge.

"Wait," you said, raising your hand, "don't cry. I'm going to distract you."

But it was too late, I was crying. As the kids said, I was fed up with him being gone, plain fed up.

"Did you ever go to boarding school?" you asked.

"No."

"I did."

You sat up straighter and put your glass down. You'd found your strand.

6

For eight years. From the age of ten to the age of eighteen, and that includes the year I was held back. It's a lot, eight years. A whole chunk of childhood and adolescence. An entire adolescence spent just counting the days. Makes for a good start in life, don't you think? I'm from a military family. Army. First Parachute Hussar Regiment. One ancestor fought at Valmy, another at Sevastopol, a great-uncle at Verdun, and both grandfathers in the Ardennes in May 1940. Hard to find a finer military pedigree. *Omnia si perdas famam servare memento.* 'If you have lost everything, remember there is honor.' That's their motto. Really sets the tone, doesn't it? My name is Mathilde but my mother really had to fight to get her way with the name because Saint Matilda was a Kraut. Fortunately the priest at the time gave his blessing, otherwise I'd have been stuck with Thérèse or Bernadette. They sent me to boarding school when I was ten. I was hardworking and was already a year ahead, so when I was ten, out you go, into the fire. My two brothers, Georges and Michel . . . All the men in my family are called either Georges or Michel because they're the two patron saints of the family business. Georges is the one in armor who slays the dragon and Michel is the paratrooper who strikes his enemies with thunder, falling out of the sky and . . . uh . . . Where was I? Oh, yes, they sent me to boarding school because my two brothers had been there before me and, as my father reminded me so I'd stop crying, it didn't kill them. So how can

a little soldier possibly reply to that? The thing is, military families move around a lot, so a boarding school is a good option
because it provides stability. *Stability*, get it? Makes you well-
balanced. Gives you a solid foundation in life. Structure. They
stick you in there and you grow up in the mold and you take
the exact shape of the mold, that way, nothing protrudes, and
afterwards you're just the right size and caliber to fit perfectly
into the barrel of the cannon. To get married, in other words.
To find yourself a handsome little junior officer and produce a
flock of little paratroopers for France. Well, I shouldn't dismiss
the entire lot. It's a world unto itself and, like everywhere,
there are good people and there are jerks. And besides, I'll
gladly confess that I met a lot of really good people from that
milieu, really sincere, fine people. But you see, the other day I
was listening to the philosopher Élisabeth de Fontenay on the
radio, there was this debate about bullfighting, and everything
she said to condemn it made such an impression on me that I
listened to it over again on the podcast so that I could copy out
what she said. Wait, don't move."

You got up, took a notebook from your bag, and came and
sat back down, not tucking your legs up, this time. And you
read, out loud:

"'Aristocratic morality, military honor, the honor of one's
name . . . Philosophy caused me to break with all that. That's
it. So I cannot accept this vast system of ethical justification
you describe, where you refer to these values: I insist that they
are no longer valid. This doesn't mean we mustn't have a sense
of honor, I try to have one, but that we must accept that this
model of virility, of courage, of mastery, is a model that has had
its day, and it has had its day precisely because of the crimes of
the twentieth century.' Thank you, Élisabeth. Thank you, gra-
cious lady. You've hit the nail on the head. And I spent my

entire childhood immersed in all that. In that model, in those outdated values. I was sent to boarding school 'for my own good' and my mother was not at all sad to see me go, since she still had my four younger siblings to wean and another child on the way, so she had enough on her hands as it was. And what was more, she said that she had very good memories of her time at convent school, that she'd made lifelong friends and that . . . in short, who cares. But it didn't suit me at all. In the early years I would go home every weekend, but then they moved to Pau and I only went home during vacation, and then they were in New Caledonia so that meant Christmas, and that was it. But by then, in any case, it was already too late. The harm was done, it didn't hurt anymore. Why am I telling you all this? Because . . . Hey, give me some more of your magic potion, would you . . . Because boarding school completely conditioned my relationship with the passage of time. With time, period. For me, time, the kind in the hourglass, is the enemy. It's the enemy, it's boredom, it's regression. I tried to move beyond the pain, but . . . no, wait, I'm getting ahead of myself. Do you remember that nursery rhyme, Solomon Grundy, Born on a Monday, Christened on Tuesday, and so on and so forth, I'll effing burst your eardrums with the thing all the way to Sunday. Do you know it? I hate that rhyme, and whenever I hear it, I go ballistic. This is how a week goes, for me—and I think that a lot of people who've been through the boarding school mill and who weren't armed for it must feel the same: on Monday, you're sad, but you still have a little of the warmth of home stored up, so you're okay, you can get by on what you have in reserve. Already by Tuesday, it's a little harder to breathe . . . because it's still just the beginning of the week, you know. By Wednesday it sucks, but for everyone else, *outside*, Wednesday is a great day, no school in the afternoon, so there are cartoons on TV, activities, dance, horseback riding, friends, music, all sorts of stuff. For them Wednesdays are great. A fine day. And it's a break in the week. When you're at boarding school, Wednesday afternoon smells of mold. Of damp. It smells like feet. You're stuck in this communal life and communal life is everything I can't stand. On Wednesday you're all crammed in there doing everything together, even being bored. Especially being bored, and it's really depressing. Debilitating. There's this military joke that goes, 'At the barracks we don't do anything, but we do it early and all together.' Well, that's exactly it. On Wednesdays and weekends when you've been left behind, you end up doing nothing, and on top of it you can see in your classmates' eyes how droopy and resigned and ungrateful you've become. You're there and you're useless. And life is useless. Life is elsewhere. Life is happening elsewhere. Fashion, music, love stories, intrigues of the sort Whatshername told me to tell you to ask Whatshisname if he wants to go out with her, giggles, kisses, betrayals, shopping, ice skating, memories . . . All of that was going on without us. For a start, it doesn't jibe with your parents' beliefs, and anyway you're in the clink, so that way it's all taken care of. Well, of course, they do have all these good works for you to contribute to if you're in need of entertainment. You can keep busy that way if you want. You can go and sing at the old people's home, you can help the old nuns to polish their priedieux, you can go and cheer up sick parishioners or, better still, even more fun, the moribund old nuns. That's where you hit the jackpot. When little virgins play hopscotch, it's only one short hop to heaven. At Christmastime they give you this sort of parcel that has everything in it at once. Just add some indigestion from milk chocolate and overlong mass and there you have it, your lovely Advent calendar. Oh, I got sidetracked—what day was I on?"

"Wednesday."

"Ah yes, thanks. So Wednesday in the cooler meant potato peeling. Thursday . . . Thursday was even worse. The longest day of the week. On Thursdays, if you didn't have a good book to read after lights out you might as well go hang yourself. You could go and receive communion. By Friday, things were looking up again. During recess you would stand there motionless gazing at the birds in the distance and hoping to see something green. On Friday you were inching your way back onto solid ground. Saturday morning you . . . Hey, you're smiling! That's great! I like making you smile. I'm glad."

"Saturday morning, you did what?"

I was smiling. And this was new. And it felt good. I hadn't smiled like that in ages. I was smiling and I began to cry like a baby. Smiling meant I could cry, at last. Not just a bitter little tear like a moment before or at the café that morning, but a wash of big greasy wet tears, plump and warm. My body letting go. Hardness yielding. Sorrow melting. It was the first time I had wept in anyone's presence. The first time in one year, two months, and five days. Because my love had killed himself all alone, I would not allow myself to weep for him in public. I had never broken down in front of anyone, ever. Why, I don't know. Out of loyalty, I think. To vindicate him. To vindicate *myself*. To convince myself that I had understood and forgiven him. I had the right to curse and insult him, but only in private. There, I could. There, when I was alone with him and had had one too many, he would get an earful, but that night, with you . . . With you telling me these really off-the-wall things, so unusual and exotic, to me, the only child of two intellectual, liberal, gentle, pacifist parents . . . Yes, it was so exotic. I could allow myself to cry in your presence, I had nothing to fear. We had not been living on the same planet, we had not been raised on the same mother's milk, we had not been fed on the same saints yet we were equally cynical. And equally modest. And tender. Besides, you hadn't known him, and . . . And I was crying. Pouring out all that pent-up sorrow. Dumping ballast. Opening the floodgates. I had permission at last.

How good it felt.

"Hey," you protested, "this is just the preamble. The sad part comes later. Keep a few tears for later, otherwise you won't be as sympathetic as you should and I'll be disappointed."

"Okay," I said, blowing my nose into my sleeve, "okay. Well then . . . Saturdays?"

"I'd rather . . . Shit, not everybody is lucky enough to be a widow! So on Saturday morning you take the train with your huge bundle of dirty laundry and come home to this noisy, lively household, but in fact they were pretty indifferent. It's not that you aren't loved . . . Oh. Right away the big words. Not that you weren't made to feel welcome, but it was like Wednesday afternoons: life went on without you. Life didn't wait for you and now no one really knew what to do with you underfoot. No, they haven't forgotten you, but someone—a niece, a cousin, a colonel's wife—has been sleeping in your bed while you were away and no one had seen fit to change the sheets, or maybe they had piled some boxes in your room, and then there was a sewing machine on your desk, they were going to take it out but they hadn't had time, so just go ahead and take it out and put it in your brother's room. Okay, it was no big deal, really, but it was worse than that, it meant you no longer had your own space anywhere on this planet. Not to mention the fact that Saturday afternoon they would often saddle you with a little sister or two little brothers to babysit, that's not the way they put it but at the end of the day that's what you were stuck with. Saturday evenings could be fun. Credit to big families where credit is due: this crowd at the dinner table, the warmth of it, laughter, arguments, the pleasure of seeing people again, good food, cakes, all the extra leaves we had to add to the table because if there was room for ten, there was room for twelve, and when there was room for twelve, there was room for twenty. Yes, twenty people at the dinner table on weekends, that would be a good average. Among neighbors, cousins, friends, family, scouts, scout leaders, my brothers' friends, red berets, green berets, seminarians, old maids, the homeless, the pious, the people who were alone in the world, lepers, and all the clan, meals at my home, whether on Saturdays or Sundays, were always special. It was like at boarding school, only you weren't wearing navy blue, the food was better, and the people spoke louder. But no sooner have we cleared the table than it's Sunday already . . . Sunday morning means mass and Sunday afternoon you're already packing again, thinking about all the homework you haven't done and will have to catch up on, on the train. And then it starts all over again. Every week the same. For eight years. That's what my childhood was like. And when there was no family home left to go to, I had to widen my circle, but at the same time I had even less privacy. I went to my grandparents', or uncles' and aunts', stayed in guest rooms at the friends of friends', and so on. For eight years, all I ever did was count the days and live with my butt between two beds. For eight years all I wanted was more stability, more sweetness in my life . . . yes, sweetness. More selfishness. A life of my own. A life I could have wrapped my arms around and said: this is mine, this is my home, don't come in. And if I let you in, then you have to do things my way and never, ever, ask me what day of the week it is. Do you follow? Does this make sense? You know, I'm not telling you all this shit so you'll feel sorry for me. I'm telling you so you'll realize how unhappy I am."

Silence.

"Am I boring you?" You were worried.

"No, not at all."

"Then help me. Because I'm not really sure I want to go on, to be honest . . . "

"Do you or don't you?"

Silence.

"I do. And I want a smoke. Do you have any nibbles?"

"You can smoke if you want."

"No. I'm trying to stop. Have you got any walnuts? Or almonds? Or sunflower seeds or something that is long and annoying to pick at?"

"Uh . . . no. I have some cereal, if you want. Honey Pops or Chocapic."

"Perfect. I'll go for the Chocapic."

"No milk, though!" you called, when I was already in the kitchenette, wondering whether I dared come back with another bottle.

I didn't dare.

Right. Two bowls of Chocapic without milk. Milk-free diet for the war wounded of the Panthéon. Change the pediment on that noble building so it reads, "To the great ladies, from the grateful psychiatric profession."

I sat back down across from you, we nibbled in silence, and then I helped you.

"Go on, then. Tell me why you're unhappy."

So, so . . . why am I unhappy? Let's see, then . . . "

And as you still couldn't go on with the next part of the story, I put some water on to boil, and placed a cup of herbal tea at your feet, by Oum-Popotte's paws.

"Thanks."

And as you seemed to have so many reasons to be unhappy that you didn't even know where to begin, I pulled on another strand of yarn for you.

"You text a lot in the morning, don't you?"

"That's it," you said with a smile, "yes, you got it."

"Are you in love?"

"Yes. No. Yes. Why are you smiling?"

"Because that's a good start!"

"Say, do you have any cigarettes?"

"I do. I don't smoke, but I have some. They were here when I moved in, they might not be any good."

"No problem. I'll have one."

I handed you the old packet of Marlboros which had been drying out under my stuffed piranha.

"Great. Thanks."

"Hey, do you mind if I pour the last of the whisky into my tea?"

"Go right ahead. Make yourself at home."

"Thanks."

You gave a sigh of wonder and relief as you let out a long puff of stale nicotine, while I swapped one hot drink for another; where there's a will, there's a way.

So then I started laughing. And I knew you were becoming my friend. Because smiling was one thing, but laughing . . . Laughing was so unexpected, as activities went, at this time of my life. So unexpected.

"I'll tell you. I'm unhappy because I'm weak, and I'm weak because I'm . . . I don't know . . . other than 'dumb' I don't know what to call it . . . This contempt I feel for my youth, those years of garrison and barracks and fucking standing around waiting, yes, all those hollow years, it's not just that I can't move beyond them, I've gone and put myself back in there. Listen, it's worse than that: I'm now living in the hollowness of those hollow years. Such a shitty, stupid thing, downright degrading. Yes, that's it, degrading. I've just realized what it means, dishonorable. Damn, what a horrible thing to realize. I've lost everything and I don't even have my honor anymore. But how did I manage to do such a thing, I wonder . . . "

Silence.

"Can you tell me?"

Silence.

"Because I don't know. I'm a bad soldier."

"Is he married?"

"Ah, you see," you winced, "on top of being dishonorable, it's banal. It's banal, conventional, vulgar. The whole nine yards. Total debacle. I'll tell you one thing, Saint Georgie and Saint Mickey must not be very proud of their little recruit. That's all there is to it: he's married. What more can I say? Nothing. Don't you have a deck of cards or some board game so we can finish this lovely little evening in a nice quiet way? Monopoly, or Pay Day?"

"I've got Uno."

"Oh, no, that's way too hard. I'll never manage."

Smiles.

"You know," I went on, "I think you're beautiful. No, wait, I don't *think* you're beautiful, you *are* beautiful. To me you don't look at all like a woman who's lost her honor. When I see you chatting with him in the morning, I see a woman who is loved, that much is completely obvious."

"Thank you. That's sweet. Sweet, and true. Or at least I think it's true. And that's the worst thing about it. I may have lost my honor, but I've still got love. Well . . . love . . . A little bit of love. What's left of it, anyway. Skewed, utterly vague, stolen text messages. It used to be I couldn't wait for the weekend and now it's the other way around. Now I dread it. Hate it, even. It's a sort of extinction, a little death. I die, and then I'm reborn, every five days. It's exhausting. It's exhausting and above all utterly pointless. I told you, what I'm going through is as negative as it gets. In the old days I used to start breathing again on Friday afternoon, and now by Thursday evening I start to fade. And over the weekend I sleep as much as possible so it will go by faster. It's cruel, isn't it? It is. Cruel. Mean. I hear God sniggering and saying, You weren't kind to the nuns? You didn't hold the rosary for the dying? You didn't finish your soy lecithin chocolates? Well here. Take this. Expiate. Go ahead and cry. Spend the Lord's day in tears and the rest of your life in the visiting room, my girl. Let that be a lesson to you.

"I don't live with a man, I live with my phone. My entire life revolves around this little slab of plastic. A sort of capricious, sadistic Aladdin's lamp that governs my mood depending on whether I rub it and it fulfills my wishes or I respect it and it abandons me. An Aladdin's lamp made in China and containing a good genie, no, a bad one, a good-for-nothing genie, a sort of bureaucrat who's only there during business hours and for whom you don't even exist under your true identity. When

I say 'I love you' it's not me saying it, it's some fraudulent identity I'm going around under these days . . . it changes so often . . . and I can't even write 'I love you' because everything is coded, as if I were his secretary doing his filing. I love you is 'Confirmed,' 'I'm thinking about you' is 'Pending,' and 'I want you' is 'Urgent.' Pretty pathetic, huh?

"Pathetic. It's not a love affair I'm having, I spend my life filing. What was the point of all those years I spent studying, anyway . . . "

"What did you study?"

"Urban planning. I have a degree from the École nationale supérieure in Paris, with honors, and why did I go through all that? To set my heart on a man with whom I'll never be able to build anything. Hey, you have to admit I'm really pretty stupid, when it comes down to it . . . "

"Why are you so categorical? Maybe he will . . . I don't know . . . change his life."

"No. Do you know of any men who leave their wives for their mistresses? When they have small children? And a loan? And an Audi? And a dog? And a dwarf bunny? And guilt? And a family home in La Trinité? No, of course you don't. I may not be clever, but I'm lucid. And besides, he's never promised me a thing. In that respect I cannot fault him. And anyway I don't fault him, for anything, when I found him he was married, and I went ahead, knowing full well what I was getting into. He has never promised me anything but never hidden anything, either. He's been honest, and that's it. But would he ever take his custom elsewhere, no, I don't believe he would. Or I no longer believe. Women are the ones who will take that kind of risk, men, never. Why? I don't know. Maybe women have more imagination . . . Or maybe they are more willing to gamble . . . Or they're on better terms with life. It's surely wrong of me to make these sweeping statements but when I look around me, that's what I see. That we are not at all equal in our dealings with life. With death, even. Women are not as afraid of death. Is that because they give life—is that the reason? I don't know. It all sounds like such a cliché but I can't think of any other explanation. Whatever they do, whatever they decide, whatever they destroy and toss to the ground, I get the impression that life is still on the side of women. Like some sort of huge house pet that always stays with the hand that feeds it even if it's the most brutal, uncaring hand. You know, it's like those old soldiers in the days of empire, like Napoleon's old guard, following him into the depths of winter and of his madness without ever questioning a single order for even one second. *The Memoirs of Sergeant Bourgogne*, have you ever read that? My godfather gave it to me when I was fifteen. It's terrific . . . Yes, men have it rough, but that's the way it is. And my lover is no more—I was going to say, 'courageous,' but that's not it, he is courageous, in his way—he's just no more robust than anyone else because he doesn't want . . . doesn't want to go against life, rub it the wrong way, displease it, be deprived of it and die one night all alone, with his mouth open. And the thing that is really twisted about all this is that if I stay with him, the age I am now, I may never have any children. That would be a shame, after all, wouldn't it? Even if I often deny it, I would like to have children. Yes, I would. Sometimes I stop thinking about it, but when I saw your kids at the café last month, it really hit me. Besides, I don't know if you noticed, but on the days that followed I didn't go to the café. I didn't want to see you again, you or the kids, I was too envious. Yes, that's it: envious. And envy is a luxury I can ill afford if I want to go on getting up in the morning. You see, I'm unhappy because everything I'm going through right now reminds me of my childhood, of how helpless I was and . . . "

You fell silent, looked up, and asked me, staring me straight in the eye:

"Can I go on?"

"You can go on."

"I feel like I'm taking advantage. Using you. Lying here on your sofa and dumping my cartload of shit on your head."

"You think you're on a sofa?"

She didn't answer.

"Come on, Mathilde . . . you can see for yourself it's not a sofa. It's Oum-Popotte's belly."

"I beg your pardon?"

"Oum-Popotte, the invisible dog's friend. The children will introduce you to him someday, you'll see . . . "

Smiles.

"And besides, you're not dumping anything, you're telling a story. You're setting yourself free. Unburdening yourself. That's much nicer."

"Thanks."

"You're welcome. It does me good, you know. It's the first time in months that I've spent the evening with someone besides myself and you have no idea how much I needed this. Go on. Tell me more, like the kids say, tell me more."

"I don't know what else to say."

"How long have you known each other?"

"Nearly four years."

"And you have no hope that the situation will, uh, evolve?"

"Do you want to help me to bump off his wife?"

"No," I said with a smile, "no. Before, I had no opinion, but now I'm against death. I have discovered that it, too, is disappointing and pointless. Really pointless. But . . . "

"But what?"

"Well, let's stop talking about him and get back to you. I don't care about him. I don't like him. I don't respect him. I don't want you to talk about him. He doesn't interest me. It's not your situation that is vulgar, it's him. I don't like liars. I don't like men who make women unhappy. I don't like men who cheat on their wives. Careful, I'm not talking about sex, here. Sex is another compartment. I'm for physical exultation and against frustration but that's something else. This is about four years, and four years means an affair. And the very word, 'affair,' is horrible. It's like 'mistress,' it's ugly. You said just now that life was more loyal to women. Life, maybe, but society, no. Society already has a connotation for everything, the bitch. And has done for centuries. On the one hand, you have Marguerite Duras's lover, this handsome Chinese man who fucks like a god, and on the other hand you have Barbey d'Aurevilly's old mistress, where she's an older woman who is always breaking his balls. Hey. Great. Thanks, Andrew Marvell, thanks. Stuff you and your world enough and time. A lover is a fine thing and it remains a charming word. *Lover man oh where can you be*, all those Billie Holiday songs. A lover is always sexy, but a mistress . . . A mistress, just the word, it reeks already of trouble and mothballs. It's so unfair. No, the problem isn't him, it's you. Why do you put up with it? Why do you go along with it? And why all that 'preamble,' that's the word you used, just to start talking about him? It's disturbing. Why did you feel you had to tell me all about your years at boarding school just so you could get to your . . . to his kid's dwarf bunny?"

"To establish a parallel."

"You think so? But you are just as responsible as he is for the situation, and surely even more so, because I expect you've tried to leave him already, haven't you?"

"Two hundred times."

"So you went back, two hundred times, too."

"Yes."

"So you see, you're the one who's calling the shots, after all. This is no parallel, it's a circle. You said so yourself, that you 'put yourself back in there,' and this is where your story gets interesting. Forget the Audi and Ye Olde Hovel by the seaside, who gives a damn. You are worth so much more than that. You are absolutely lovely, and funny, and tender, you're sensitive and intelligent, you know the difference between Wigglytuff and Jigglypuff, you've almost quit smoking, you are one of the most attractive women I've ever met and you know damn well you would have no trouble at all seducing anyone who catches your eye, so why this . . . this life 'standing around waiting,' to quote you once again? It must be that deep down it suits you, it really does, isn't that it? There are loads of plus sides to standing around waiting. You don't have to think, you don't have to take any initiative, you obey, you can be passive . . . You're in such a repetitive, repressive situation that there's no room for doubt or anxiety, and I mean anxiety with a capital A, existential anxiety, and obviously that is very convenient, but it leaves no room for adventure, for meeting people, for chaos and confusion, for fate, in other words . . . For the whims and twists of fate. That's a really practical setup you've got. Real cozy. You're like a duty officer in his little shack, you don't have to question a thing, you don't ask yourself any questions, and often, basically, this duty officer doesn't even give a damn about what it is he's guarding. He could give a flying fuck. He's just there freezing his balls off until the next bozo takes over. And so, why not? But then don't go telling me that women are on better terms with life, because honestly, Mathilde, you . . . you have let me down, there . . . "

"Are you a shrink or something?"

Your voice suddenly became more aggressive.

"No, not at all. I'm just trying to understand. If you hadn't started by telling me about your childhood, I might be giving you a different speech, but because you did, I find it troubling, don't you? It's not the fact that you spent years in . . . on your military base that decides who you are or who could make you who you are, it's the fact that you needed to tell me about them in such detail. Listening to you I get the impression that you have deliberately chosen to live your life as a sort of perpetual Wednesday afternoon, and I would like to know why. I'm not judging you, I hope that's clear? I'm just trying to understand."

"You mean I'm suffering from Stockholm syndrome or some putrid thing like that?"

"I don't know, it's not like your years in boarding school can be compared to being taken hostage, but you have to admit it's a tempting explanation. You tell me that for eight years you had no life, and now that you're grown up, emancipated, and free, you go and add four more years to the bag. Hey, admit you like counting the days, don't you? What other explanation could there be?"

You sat there, silent.

"I've offended you," I said. "Forgive me. I can see it on your face, what I've said is offensive. Forgive me. I have no right—"

"No, no. You haven't offended me at all. On the contrary, it's as if you're disinfecting me. I'm not being reticent, it's just that it stings. What you're doing is painful. It's surely doing me good, but it is painful."

"Are you sure you don't want to play Uno?"

Smiles.

"No. I want to go on. I want you to go on examining this wound with me. Do you mind?"

"I'm listening."

"No, I'm listening to you."

"But I have nothing to tell you, you know . . . "

"You do. Of course you do. You have to tell me to leave him, once and for all."

"But I don't need to tell you that, you know it already! You've said as much yourself. By coming here, for a start. It's not a story, your confession, it's a geological survey map. That smartphone you peck at like a wretch; the way you deny reality; the way you can only speak of tenderness if you smuggle it

in, all those stories about files to organize, or rotten foundations, or building permits you'll never get, those were all your
words. That's your vision of things. Your own conclusions.
You've never once talked about how good this man makes you
feel, have you?"

Silence. Stinging.

"He does do you good," I continued, more gently, "I know
he does. I just told you how pretty you looked, those mornings
when you had the time to talk to him, but that sort of thing
won't do, Mathilde, it just won't do. It's too brief. Too
restricted. Too stingy. We all know that real happiness doesn't
exist, and we have to do what we can to get by without it, but
in this instance . . . This thing of yours is a real trap. To love a
man for four years and at the end of all these years you still
have to write 'confirmed' instead of 'I love you,' that is . . . Yes.
You're right. It's the end of honor."

Silence.

I poured the last drop of whiskey into your cold cup.

"Thank you," you murmured, your head down.

"You can't go on playing this game, can you?"

"I can't leave him. Every time I try, I go to pieces. Maybe
life is stingy with him but without him it's even worse."

"Life? What life? Four years leading this clandestine life.
Four years in hiding. Like some resistance fighter in the
Maquis. Four years of sorrow over a man who can only hold
you in his arms at the price of a lie, and who thinks it's enough
to toss you a handful of text messages now and again. But, hey,
remember: you're not a whore, Mathilde, you're not a whore.
I know you're in pain. I know that. But the twisted thing is that
all you have to show for four years in the shadow of a married
man is an accumulation of false joy, false starts, false intimacy,
pretend reunions, disappointment, humiliation, and bitterness,
and at the end of it all, you've lost yourself along the way. You
can't even remember that you are worth a thousand times

more than anything this man can give you. Take that back: not give you."

"No. Don't say that. It's not true. He's better than that. You don't know him but he's better than what you say he is. Otherwise I wouldn't have come this far."

"Does he know you want a child?"

"He suspects as much."

"And he won't give you one?"

"No."

"If he really loved you, he would leave you. When you love a woman who wants a child, you give her one or else you let her go."

"*You give her one.* What a macho thing to say. You sound like some shitty little adjutant."

"I'm talking like a mom. But it is macho, I'll give you that. Okay, *You want to have children with her or else you let her go.*"

"And now you sound like a priest."

"I sound like the widow of a man who was twenty years older than me, and who didn't want children, who thought he was too old to be a father, so he left me, then came back one year later, and stood there waiting for me when I got off work, pushing a beautiful baby carriage in front of him. A Bonnichon baby carriage, no less. But for a whole year, not a single sign of life. Ever. No text messages, no flowers, no notes, nothing. For a whole year I was free."

Silence.

"I'm afraid to leave him. I'm afraid of solitude. I'm afraid I'll regret it, and miss him. I'm afraid I'll never live so fully again. I'm afraid of being bored and never getting over it. Even if I stop myself from thinking like this, I'm sure there's some mean little bug deep inside me, some sort of termite, that still believes he'll eventually leave his wife, even though they've just bought an apartment together. In fact, I'm hanging on for all the wrong reasons. I'm hanging on because I'm listening to that mean little bug. I'm listening to my worst side. The one that lies and fabricates, the one that is cowardly and scared."

"Following orders that bring dishonor—that's what's so tragic about the military, isn't it? Why are you still forcing yourself into this sort of dilemma? Why? You have to act like that great Élisabeth you spoke of earlier, Mathilde: leave behind these outdated values. Desert. Unharness your horse. Take off your uniform and lay down your arms. Get the hell out. Go over the wall. You deserve a better life. You know, I would never speak to you in this tone if I hadn't seen you with my kids. If I hadn't seen you sniffing their security blankets or running your hand through Alice's curls a while ago. Why risk depriving yourself of all of that, tell me? Why? For who? For what? And if you were to have a child behind his back, that would be as appalling as infidelity, so you have to make the break if you want a sweeter life some day. You have no choice. You really have to get out of there. And as I'm telling you all this I realize just how limited my words are, because . . . Because I had found him, the eternal lover, the dream daddy for my kids; I had found him. And now look . . . at the end of the day, here I am bringing them up all alone, so . . . So I should keep my mouth shut."

Laughter. Shouts. Noise.

Voices raised, and the sound of broken glass on the pavement.

"Listen," I continued, sitting up straight, "I'll tell you my truth. I'll tell you my truth that isn't your truth and which isn't reality, either. My truth is that I may be able to lecture for hours on end but I'm wrong. I'm wrong because if I'm honest, here's another truth: what the hell do I know. I've never known much, and since my love left me, I've been a complete wreck, so really, you can just take it or leave it, all this stuff I said. You know, above all, leave it. Yes, leave it, I'm in no position to go explaining life to others just now. Not only am I a complete wreck, I'm also in an even more dubious state than a wreck. I'm fallible across the board, believe me. As I sit here talking to you there is nothing solid about me, nothing. But what I can add, uh, to keep playing my part as anesthesiologist, so to speak, is that when I met him, I was the one who was married, well, not officially, but as good as. Yes. I was the one causing the pain. He was so clever that he never had to put any pressure on me, naturally. Not the slightest pressure, no, and he would never have dared talk down to me the way I just have to you. This lecture I just gave you—he would have been horrified to hear me talking like that. Horrified and disappointed. He thought I was more subtle than that. What he did, to get me to leave my little shack that was as dreary as it was comfortable, what he did is he let me go on and on about my life with my ex—my domestic partner—how he loved to whisper the phrase, dragging out the second syllable to the tip of my dimples, he would let me go on and on, like you have this evening, listening to me very attentively, as I have this evening, and then at the end he . . . "

Silence. I was smiling.

"He what?"

"He yawned. He yawned and it made me laugh."

"And then?"

"And then nothing. And then I left a man I was bored with for a man who made me laugh."

"Whoa . . . " you groaned, curling up in the folds of our confessional, "I would have loved to have known him . . . Tell me about him. Tell me some more about him."

"No. Some other day. Some other night. We have to get to sleep now. School day tomorrow."

"No, tell me. Tell me something. Please. Tell me another nice thing to add some grist to your mill and give me strength."

"Another time, I promise."

Silence.

"Do you mind if I sleep here for a few hours?"
"No, of course not. Wait, I'll find you a blanket."

I got back up, threw out the last empty bottle, put our cups and bowls in the sink, went to get a comforter from the bed and came back, closed the shutters, pulled the curtains, turned up the heat, and tucked you in.

I switched off the light then added:

"If I had known I loved him that much, I would have loved him even more."

Did that thing, that grist, those last words murmured in the dark, give you courage?

I don't know. In the morning, you had already struck camp and I never saw you again.

MY DOG IS DYING

There came a day when he couldn't even get up in the truck on his own. He didn't even pretend to try. He sat down next to the running board and waited for me. Hey, I said, get a move on there, old boy. But the look he gave me, I hung my head. I lifted him up into his spot and he lay down as if it was no big deal, but that day I stalled when I tried to start up the truck.

Only us two in the waiting room. Holding him like this so tight but trying not to squeeze, it's giving me shooting pains in my shoulder. I go over to the window to show him the view and even then, even now, I can tell it interests him.

Little snoop . . .

I rub his head with my chin and murmur:

"What am I gonna do without you, huh? What am I gonna do?"

He closes his eyes.

I called my boss before coming. I told him I'd be late for my shift, but that I'd make it up. That I always make it up. That he oughta know, after all these years.

"What's up?"

"I've got a problem, Monsieur Ricaut."

"Nothing mechanical, I hope?"

"No, no, it's my dog."

"What's wrong with the mutt this time? Get stuck in some chicken's ass or something?"

"No, it's not that, it's . . . I have to take him to the vet, 'cause this is the end, now."

"The end of what?"

"The end of his life. And since they don't open until nine, by the time they do it and all, I'll be late to the depot. That's why I'm calling."

"Oh, shit. I'm sorry to hear that, Jeannot. We liked your dog. What happened to him?"

"Nothing. Nothing happened. He's just old."

"Oh, shoot. That's gonna be rough on you, that's a tough one. How long have you had him on your truck?"

"Ages."

"And what were you supposed to do this morning?"

"Garonor."

"What was it? Stuff to Deret's?"

"Yeah."

"Listen, Jeannot, you know what? Take the day off, okay? We'll manage."

"You can't manage without me. The kid's on leave and Gérard is at traffic school."

"Oh, of course . . . That's right. But still, we'll manage. I'll do it for you. It'll oil the machinery a little. It's been such a long time I don't even know if my arms are long enough to reach the wheel!"

"Are you sure?"

"'Course I'm sure, don't worry. Take the day off, it's fine."

Last year in September, when there were the roadblocks, the strikes really messed things up and they gave me a hard time because I didn't want to join in with the others. They asked me if I liked sucking the boss's cock. I remember, it was Waldek who said it and even today I often think about what he said. But I didn't want to go on strike. I didn't want my wife to be all alone at night, and to be honest, I didn't really believe in any of that anymore. It was over. It was too late. I told my co-workers that old Ricaut was just as much up shit creek as we were and I didn't want to go acting like a clown at the tollbooths while guys from Geodis or Mory's were taking over our markets. And besides, and I'll say it straight up, I've always respected the man. As bosses go, he's always treated us fair. And even today, with my dog dying, he's treating me fair.

I say my dog because he doesn't have a name, otherwise I'd call him by his name. It was so I wouldn't get so attached, but even now it's the same as with everything, at the end of the day I got screwed all the same.

I found him one night in the middle of August on my way back from Orléans. On the Route Nationale 20, just before Étampes.

I was sick of living.

Ludovic had left us a few months earlier and if I was still on this earth shifting equipment and spare parts, it was 'cause I'd worked it out that it would take me eight more years of active employment for my wife to get a halfway decent pension.

Those days, my truck was my prison. I even bought myself one of those little calendars where you peel the days off one by one so that it would be dead clear in my head: eight years, I said, over and over, eight years.

Two thousand, nine hundred and twenty days, then *adios*.

I didn't listen to the radio anymore, I never took anyone along for the ride, I never felt like talking anymore, and when I went home it was so I could switch on the box. My wife was already in bed. Should mention she took a lot of pills in those days.

I smoked.

Two packs of Gauloises a day, and I would sit there thinking about my dead son.

I could hardly sleep, I never finished the food on my tray, I threw out the food and I wanted it all to end. Or to go backwards. To do things differently. So that his mother wouldn't be in so much pain. So she'd finally put away her damn brooms. I wanted to go back to a time when it might still have been possible for her to get the hell away from our home. I clenched my jaw so hard that one night I broke a tooth, just thinking about it.

They made me go to the company doctor to get some antidepressants (Ricaut was worried I'd screw up in one of his trucks), and while I was getting dressed the guy said:

"Look, I don't know precisely what is going to kill you. I don't know whether it will be sorrow, cigarettes, or the fact that you haven't been eating properly for months, but one thing is for sure, if you go on in the state you're in today, well, rest assured, Monsieur Monati, rest assured: you will not be long for this world."

I didn't answer. I needed the certificate for Dany, the secretary, so I let him talk and then I left. I bought the medication so that everything would be A-OK with the insurance and social security and then I threw the pills in the garbage.

I didn't want them, and as for my wife, I was afraid she'd use them to do herself in.

It was a lost cause, anyway. I'd had my fill of doctors. I couldn't stand the sight of them anymore.

The door opens. It's our turn. I say I've come to have my dog put to sleep. The vet asks me if I want to stay. I say yes and he goes off into another room. He comes back with a syringe filled with some pink liquid. He explains that the animal won't suffer, that for him it will be like falling asleep and . . . Save your breath, pal, I feel like saying, save your breath. My kid left before me too, so you know—just save your breath.

*

I began smoking like a chimney and my wife never stopped cleaning. From morning to night and eight days a week, that's all she could think of: cleaning.

It started when we got back from the cemetery. We had family, cousins on her side who'd come up from the Poitou, and as soon as they'd taken their last bite she threw them all out. I thought it was so she could have some peace and quiet but no, she reached for her apron and tied herself up in it.

She hasn't taken it off since.

In the beginning I thought, hey, it's normal, she's keeping busy. I don't talk much, and she keeps moving. Everyone does what they can to deal with the pain. It will pass.

But I was wrong. Nothing passed.

Nowadays at our place you can lick the floor if you want. The floor, the walls, the doormat, the steps, and even the toilets. Never fear, it's all been pickled in bleach. Before I've even finished wiping my plate with the bread she's already rinsing it off and if God forbid I put my knife on the table I can clearly see her biting her tongue to keep from telling me off. I always take my shoes off at the door and even my slippers, I can hear her slapping them together the minute I've got my back turned.

One night when she was still on all fours scouring the grout lines in the floor tiles, I got mad:

"Dammit, Nadine, will you stop that, for pity's sake! Stop! You're going to drive me crazy!"

She looked at me, didn't answer, and went back to her scraping.

I tore the sponge from her hand and hurled it to the other side of the room.

"Stop it, I said."

I almost felt like killing her.

She stood up straight, went to get her sponge, and started again.

From that day on I slept in the basement, and when I brought the dog home I didn't even give her time to react:

"He'll live downstairs. He won't come up. You'll never see him. He'll be on the truck with me."

Often, a thousand times, even, I wanted to take her in my arms and squeeze her, or shake her like a doll and beg her to stop all that cleaning. Beg her. Tell her I was here, too, and that I was just as miserable as she was. But it just wasn't going to happen: there was always a vacuum cleaner or a basket of dirty laundry in the way.

There were times I didn't feel like going to bed all alone. Sometimes I'd hang around, drinking, and fall asleep in front of the box.

I was waiting for her to come and get me.

But she never came. And eventually I accepted it. I'd put the cushions back where they belonged and go down to my basement, almost breaking my neck on the stairs.

When everything was so clean that she couldn't find even the tiniest speck of dust, she went and bought a Kärcher and started on all the masonry and outside walls. Even when the neighbor who works in construction warned her that she'd ruin the mortar, she kept on cleaning.

On Sundays, she leaves her house alone. On Sundays she takes her rags and all her cleaning stuff and goes to the cemetery.

She didn't used to be like that. I fell in love with her because she put me in a good mood. My papa always said: *Oh Nanni, tua moglie è une usignolo.* Your wife is a little songbird.

In the beginning when we were together, if you can believe it, she didn't bother too much with housekeeping. Not at all.

I was driving way too fast when I saw my dog for the first time. Thing is, back then the tachographs were not as precise as they are now. And there were not as many speed checks.

And I didn't give a damn anyway. I was driving a Scania 360. One of the last ones we had, I remember. It must've been around two o'clock in the morning and I was so tired I left the radio on full blast to keep me awake.

At first I only saw his eyes. Two yellow dots in the beam of the headlights. He was crossing the road and I had to swerve hard to avoid him.

I was madder than hell. Mad at him because he'd frightened me, and also mad at myself for driving like an idiot. First, I had no business going so fast, and second, it was a miracle there was nothing along the shoulder, otherwise I would have crushed everything in the way. I wasn't proud of myself. I went on cursing myself like that for a few hundred yards, swearing like some lousy truck driver, and then I wondered what the hell that mutt was doing there on the highway at two o'clock in the morning in the middle of August.

Another poor critter who wouldn't be going to the seaside with his owners . . .

I'd seen entire colonies of miserable dogs since I'd been on the road. Some of them were hurt, some dead, tied up, crazy, lost, limping, others running after vehicles, but I'd never stopped before. So? Why that one?

I don't know.

In the time it took for me to decide, I'd already gone a long ways on. I drove a little further looking for a place to turn around, but because the road was narrow, I made the stupidest maneuver of my entire career: I stopped my wagon right there, in the middle of the road. I turned on my hazards and went looking for that critter.

Death can't always win.

That was the first time I'd gotten an idea in my head since the boy passed. The first time I was making a decision that actually concerned me. I didn't really believe it.

I walked in the dark for a long time, behind the guardrail when there was one, through tall grasses and all the crap people throw out into nature. Beer cans, cigarette packs, plastic wrappers, and bottles of piss courtesy of my coworkers who are too lazy or in too much of a hurry to pull over for five minutes. I looked up at the moon behind the clouds and I heard an owl or something like that shrieking in the distance. I was wearing a short-sleeved shirt and I was beginning to feel cold. I thought, if he's still there, I'll take him, but if I can't see him from the road, forget it. Leaving the truck stopped back there with the high beams on was not a good idea. And when I reached the bend in the road that had almost brought the pair of us to grief, I saw him.

He was sitting by the side of the road, looking my way.

"Okay," I went, "you coming?"

He has trouble breathing. You can tell he's in pain. I say kind things to him, stroking the white line between his eyes. Before the needle even comes back out, I feel the weight of his head roll onto my arm and his dry nose come to land in my palm. The vet asks me if I'd rather have him cremated or send him to the slaughterhouse. I'll take him with me, I say.

"Careful, there are regulations to be followed, you know—"

I raise my hand. He says nothing more.

I have a really hard time filling out the check. The lines are dancing before my eyes and I can't remember the date.

I bundle him up in my jacket and lay him on his blanket, in his usual spot.

My wife and I wanted a second child so the little boy wouldn't be on his own, but we couldn't seem to manage.

No matter how hard we tried, all the laughs and evenings out for dinner or drinks, no matter how we counted the days and made a game of it and all the rest, every month she got her aching tummy and every month I saw she was losing a bit more confidence in us. Her sister told her to go and see a doctor and get some treatment, but I was against it. I reminded her of what she already knew, that the boy had come along fine on his own, and why would she go mess with her health taking hormones and shots all the way to kingdom come.

But with everything you hear nowadays, nuclear disasters, GMOs, mad cow disease, and all the crap they make us eat, I'm sorry I said all that to her, I'm sorry. Her organism would have been no more messed with than the next person's.

Anyway, by the time we decided, Ludovic was having his first bad spells, and from that day on we put aside any thoughts about having another kid.

From that day on, we stopped making plans.

He wasn't even two years old when he started coughing. Day and night, standing, sitting, at the dinner table, lying down, or watching his cartoons, he coughed. He coughed and couldn't breathe.

His mother went silent: she was watching. That was all she did, like an animal, just listening carefully, observing his breathing, showing her fangs.

She did the rounds of waiting rooms with her kid under her arm. She took days off. She went up to Paris. She got lost in the métro. She spent all her savings on taxi drivers, and saw a heap of specialists who made her wait longer and longer, and who got more and more expensive.

The worst of it was that she went on making herself pretty, every time. She never knew when she might happen upon the person who was going to save her little kiddywink.

He missed a lot of school. And she lost a lot in the process, too. She had a good job, they liked her at work and she got along well with her coworkers, but after a while they sent for her all the same.

They sent for her to have her sign her own walking papers.

She said she was relieved, but that night, she couldn't eat a thing. It was unfair, she said, again and again, all of it, so unfair.

She went looking for reasons for the allergy. She changed the carpet, the bedding, the curtains; no more stuffed animals, or going to the park, or sledding, or having little friends over, or petting animals, or drinking milk, or eating hazelnuts, nothing. All the things kids like best.

At first that's all she did: give him a hard time. A hard time, to save him. During the day she watched him, and at night she listened to his breathing.

Asthma.

I remember, one evening in the bathroom.

I was brushing my teeth while she was removing her makeup.

"Look at all these wrinkles," she moaned, "all this gray hair. Every day I'm older than the day before. Every night I'm getting older faster than all the other women my age. I'm tired. So, so tired."

I couldn't answer because of the toothpaste. I just shrugged my shoulders to say that was bullshit. Women's bullshit. You're beautiful. Yet it was true. She'd lost weight. Her face had changed. That softness she used to have, gone.

We made love less often, but we left the door open.

I'm driving. I don't know where I'm going to bury my dog.

This ratter, this loudmouth, this little mongrel. This pal of mine, who kept me alive so long, and was such good company. Who loved hearing Dalida sing, who was afraid of storms, who could spot a rabbit a hundred yards away, and who always slept with his head on my thigh. Yup, I don't know yet where to bury the rascal.

Thanks to him I've practically stopped smoking. Fact is, he had started sneezing too, the bastard. I know he was making fun of me, because he didn't always wait for me to light up to start his act, but anyway, it brought back too many bad memories. So I waited until I could stop for a break.

I stopped getting annoyed because the stores were about to close, or because I was having trouble parking, or because it was costing me a fortune, or because I needed change and all that. I started putting on weight, and now it was the diesel smell on my hands that bothered me, or the scent of the fields of rape we drove past, but quitting did me a lot of good. Really, really a lot. Suddenly here was the proof that I could still be a little freer than I thought.

Last thing I expected.

Thanks to my dog, I began talking again, and meeting people. I never knew so many of my fellow drivers had dogs. I learned new words, found out about new pedigrees, spouted all kinds of bullshit myself and shared bags of kibble from Pamplona to The Hague. Even when I couldn't understand a word they said I made friends with guys, I just looked at their license plates to figure out where they were from, but they were like me, they weren't as alone as they seemed.

Other drivers have their truck, their cargo, their schedule, and their stress. We have all that, but a dog to boot.

And he made friends, too. I even have a photograph of one of his puppies in the glove compartment. In Moldova, is where he is. With his owner we swore we'd recognize each other if one day we stopped in the same place to let the dogs go off to piss, but it never happened. Oh well.

Through him I met Bernard, who had lost a son, same age as ours. And Bernard, his wife left him on top of it all. Twice he tried to do himself in, but then in the end he remarried. Like he says, it's more or less the same as before except he's got more hassles to deal with now.

When we find each other at night on the radio, we talk. Well, he does most of the talking. He's a real blabber. He knows how to go about it, mixing jokes in with all the rest. And he has a nice accent, he's from the Béarn. We talk and then afterwards, with all he's told me, it keeps me awake for a long time.

Nanar64.

A friend.

Thanks to my dog, I stopped clenching my jaw and started enjoying being on the road again. Since I have to stop to take a leak every now and again, I've even seen places here and there where it would be real nice to settle down.

Thanks to this abandoned dog who waited for me like a good boy that first night, who never doubted for a moment that I would come back for him, and who could count on me ever after for his well-being, I got better. I won't say happier, but better.

My wife should have had something or someone like that.

I'm still driving. I have to find him a good spot.

In the sun. And with a view.

I don't know if this is a good memory or a bad one . . . Ludovic must have been eleven or twelve years old, skinny, white as an aspirin, tied to his mother's apron strings, whining whenever he had to make the slightest effort, missing school, excused from gym, glued to his cartoons and video games. Not a well-rounded kid, in other words.

On an evening that was different from the rest I blew a fuse.

I grabbed my wife's wrist and forced her to turn and look at her puny little boy:

"No way, Nadine! No way!" I yelled. "Is he just gonna sit there until the day we die, is that it? He has to become a man, for Chrissake! I'm not asking him to run a marathon, but come on! Is he gonna spend the rest of his life reading crap and piling up bricks on a TV screen, is that it? Shit!"

My wife began to panic and the boy sat up straight, putting down his joystick.

"Ludo, I'm not saying this to pester you, but at your age, you're supposed to go out. To make us mad at you! You have to start fiddling with a moped and looking at girls. I don't know . . . but you're not gonna learn anything about life sitting around here. Switch that thing off, son. Unplug it, right now."

"I do look at girls," he responded, with a smile.

"But just looking, that's not enough, dammit! You have to talk to them, too!"

"Calm down, Jean," my wife begged, "calm down."

"I am calm!"

"No, you're not. But you're going to stop this right away or you're going to make him have a fit."

"A fit? Now what sort of bullshit is that? Am I foaming at the mouth or something?"

"Stop. It's the stress, you know that—"

"Stress, my ass! You're making him like this, pampering him all the time. You're the one who's keeping him from growing up, just so you can keep your little doll!"

His mother burst into tears.

With her, tears used to come easily.

During the night he coughed and had to use his inhaler four times. I sleep next to the wall, I couldn't help hearing.

The next day was Sunday. She came to get me in the shed:

"He's got an appointment on Wednesday at the Necker children's hospital. You can take him this month. That way you can ask Robestier yourself when the boy can go back to training and hanging around in cafés, okay?"

"I have work on Wednesday."

"No," she went, "you don't, because your kid has to go to the hospital and you are going with him."

The look she gave me, I didn't protest. And it was true, I didn't have work on Wednesday. It was the first day of fishing season and I knew that she knew that, too.

Hey, up there, not bad . . . That little hill, there.

My dog wasn't a dog. He was a gossip, always watching what was going on. Always sitting perfectly straight, his forepaws neat and even on the dashboard, eyes on the road. Sometimes he would start to howl, God knows why. There was something in the distance he didn't like the looks of, and he controlled it all from his observation post.

Christ he could really give me an earful when I think of it . . .

People asked me: Is that a coyote you've got there for the speed checks? Yeah, sure, I'd say, a great one. On a suction cup, no less. So a hill, hell yeah . . . the least I can do.

So of course I didn't dare make a fuss. I was in awe of the other kids in the waiting room, and then of all the exams they put my Ludo through. At one point I even felt like saying, Hey, look. That's enough, now. You can see he can't take any more. Is this to humiliate him, or what? In the end they put him in this sort of glass cabin and asked him to blow into these twisted tubes until he felt dizzy. It was so they could read his breathing on a computer graph.

Like for heartbeats.

I was sitting on a stool, holding his jacket.

While the nurse was changing the tubes, I sent him little signs of encouragement. It wasn't really a competition, but he was being brave all the same.

Then he started doing what they said all over again, while I looked at all those screens trying to understand something.

An explanation for what our life had turned into. All the sleepless nights—why? All the anxiety? Why was my son always the smallest one in the class and why didn't his mother love me the way she used to? Huh? Why? Why us? But all those numbers jumping around all over the place, I couldn't understand a damn thing.

I found out she'd spoken to the doctor before the appointment because at one point he turned to me and said, with this priestly little smile:

"So, Monsieur Monati, it would seem that you are a bit . . . " (He acted as if he was hunting for the right word) " . . . a bit *put out* by your son's behavior in his day-to-day life, am I right?"

I was speechless.

"You think he's too soft?" said the doctor.

"Excuse me?"

"Abulic? Indolent? Apathetic?"

I was getting hot. I didn't understand any of the things he was saying.

"His mother's been talking to you, hasn't she? Look, Doctor, I don't know exactly what she told you, but all I want is for my kid to have a normal life. A normal life, you understand? I don't think it's doing him any favors, the way she's always waiting on him hand and foot. I know he's not a healthy boy, but I wonder if leaving him shut in at home all day long, like he's in some sort of sterilizer, isn't just making him weaker."

"I see, Monsieur Monati, I see. I understand your concerns and, I fear I am at pains to reassure you. However, I would like to suggest that you undergo a sort of little test, as well. Would you agree to that?"

Worse than a priest, an archbishop.

Ludovic was looking at me.

"Of course," I replied.

He asked me to take off my jacket. He stood up and went to get a pair of scissors from behind his computers, and he cut a wide strip of adhesive and stuck it over my mouth. I didn't like that one bit. Good thing I didn't have a cold that day. Then he went out of the room for a long time and Ludo and I found ourselves sitting there all alone like a pair of morons.

"Mhmm . . . Mhmm . . . " I went, walking like a penguin.

He laughed. When he narrowed his eyes like that, I could see his mother. Nadine, when she was younger. The same lovable little face. The same pointed little nose.

The doctor came back in with a yellow plastic straw. A kid's straw, like for drinking milkshakes. With the blade of a scalpel he made a tiny hole in front of my mouth and slid the straw through the adhesive and asked me if I could breathe. I nodded.

Then he took a needle from a syringe and pierced the straw in several places. He glanced at me. It was okay, no problem, he could go on with his stupid little game.

Then he stuck a nose clip on me and already I didn't feel so good.

I began to freak out.

He turned to the boy:

"What's your dad's name?"

"Jean. But everyone calls him Jeannot."

"I see . . . " Then he turned to me: "Are you ready, Jeannot? Follow me. Naturally, strictly no touching my little device. I can count on you, can't I?"

I pulled over, opened the trunk, took my shovel, and tucked my dead dog inside my jacket.

The weather was fine, I zipped up my jacket and off we went.

We followed the doctor down the hall and he asked us to wait for a minute. Ludo and I looked at each other, shaking our heads: Hey, who is this weirdo doctor, anyway? Well, actually, it was Ludo shaking his head; me, I couldn't. I just rolled my eyes and even that took more energy than I would have thought. After that I didn't budge an inch.

Robestier came back. He'd taken off his white coat and he was skipping like a kid, toeing an old soccer ball.

Then he kicked it toward me:

"Go, Jeannot, come on! Pass it to me!"

Not for one second did I have a hope in hell of touching that damn ball. Not one second.

I waddled a few steps, but I tried to keep from leaning forward best I could. The straw had to stay horizontal. I couldn't move my head too abruptly, especially not from left to right or up and down, otherwise I wouldn't have enough air.

But I tried.

"Hey, Jeannot, c'mon! What you doing, buddy?"

I didn't recognize him. This man who'd just acted so proud behind his desk, and now he was acting all familiar and hopping around like some bunny rabbit.

"You don't need to score a goal, but hey, c'mon! Pass it to me, at least!"

What with the straw I swore I would not spit out, the lack of air, plus my irritation at not being able to touch that damn ball, I began to lose it. I tried to stay calm, but I felt like I was going to die.

"NO, MONSIEUR MONATI! NO!"

And all I could do to keep from tearing off that goddamn adhesive, that is, to keep from losing face there in front of my kid, was to fall on the floor, curl up in a ball, and lie there motionless as long as I could with my forehead against my knees and my arms around my head to shield myself from the world.

Don't anybody look at me. Don't anybody speak to me. Don't anybody touch me. Just let me lie here playing dead as long as possible so that I can start living again.

He held out his hand and pulled me to my feet while I peeled off his confounded booby trap.

"So you see, Jean, what you just experienced, that's what this is . . . "

He pointed to his machine. The little glowing screen where

the best Ludovic could do, blowing as hard as he could, appeared in the form of a tiny spidery scrawl across a graph that was a thousand times too big for it.

I didn't think the hill would be so steep. I'm using my shovel as a walking stick and the words come back, and I say them out loud: *So, Jeannot, where's that pass? No, Monsieur Monati, no!*

That evening I went to see my kid in his room. He was in his bed, reading a magazine. I pulled the chair out from his desk.

"You okay?"

"Yeah."

"What you reading?"

He showed me the cover.

"Is it good?"

"Yeah."

"Good . . . "

I could see he didn't really feel like talking. He was tired and all he wanted was to read his thing about the ten enigmas of the solar system without being disturbed.

"You take your Ventolin?"

"Yeah."

"Okay, good . . . everything okay then?"

"Yeah."

"Am I, am I bothering you? Keeping you from reading, is that it?"

He looked me in the eyes.

"Yeah," he said, with a broad grin, "you are kinda bothering me."

Ah. When I think back. He was such a good kid. A really, really good kid.

On leaving his room I couldn't help but ask him:

"So how do you manage?"

"How do I manage what?"

"To breathe."

He put his magazine on his lap and he paused, thinking, to give me the only possible right answer:

"I concentrate."

I wished him good night and just as I was closing the door I heard him giggling:

"'Night, Ronaldo."

And just to have a little laugh like that, quietly, just to poke fun at his old dad, well, it nearly suffocated him.

The perfect spot. A sort of little outcrop facing south-southwest. He'd have plenty to see from there, my little busy-body . . .

I dug.

I left him my jacket. I took the two lumps of sugar I'd swiped from a self-service and slipped them into the inside pocket.

For the road.

Didn't take long to fill in the hole. He wasn't a big dog.

I sat down next to him and all of a sudden I felt completely alone in the world.

I smoked a cigarette, then another one, then a third one.

After that I took hold of the shovel to hoist myself back to my feet.

All the doctors kept saying we had to send Ludovic some-where with fresh air. That he had to continue his studies up in the mountains and far away from us. We had a hard time deciding what to do. Especially my wife.

In the end we enrolled him in a sort of sanatorium-high school in the Pyrenees. It went smoothly. Nadine said it was because of his good report cards. In my opinion it was mainly because of his medical records, but in the end, it hardly mattered, he was glad to be going.

He had just turned fifteen, was in tenth grade, and he was an adorable kid. I'm not saying this just because he was my kid, I'm saying it because it's true. Was it just his nature, or was it his illness that had made him like that? I have no idea, but I'll just say it one more time: he was an adorable kid.

Really small for his age, but already a fine gentleman . . .

It happened just before Easter vacation. We were waiting impatiently for him to come back. His mother was going around in circles and I'd asked for my days off. We were going to take him to the Futuroscope before heading down to his cousins' place in Parthenay. I was there when the phone rang.

The headmaster of the school informed us that our son Ludovic Monati had had an attack during recess and the administration had immediately called for an ambulance, but the boy died on his way to the nearest hospital.

The hardest thing was clearing out his room at the school. We had to take everything and put it in garbage bags: his clean clothes and his dirty clothes, his games, his books, the posters he'd hung around his bed, his notebooks, his secrets, and all his boxes of medication.

Nadine did not bat an eyelash. Her only request was not to run into the headmaster. There was something about this "sad affair," as he put it, certain details she could not stomach.

A fifteen-year-old boy doesn't just up and die like that, out in the schoolyard during recess.

When we were outside the building she turned to me and said:

"I don't want you in the way. Go and wait for me in the car. I'd rather be on my own."

She never had to repeat it and yet from that day on I have always felt like I'm in her way.

Traffic's heavy. I didn't think there would be such gridlock. I'm not used to driving at this time of day. I'm not used to feeling trapped by traffic. People honking their horns and me missing my dog.

Tomorrow I'll get back into my truck and his smell will be there.

I'll need some time to get used to not having him around.

How long?

How much longer?

How long until I stop looking over his way, asking him if everything is okay, reaching over toward the passenger seat, huh?

How long will it all take?

I said, It's me, and I went into the kitchen to pour myself a beer. I was about to go downstairs when she called out to me. She was sitting in the living room.

She wasn't wearing her apron and her coat was folded across her lap.

"I was getting worried, so I called your work and Ricaut told me about your dog."

"Oh?"

I'd already turned to go when she added:

"Do you want to go for a little walk?"

I was speechless.

"Come on, let's go. Put your shoes back on and come with me. I'm waiting."

We went out, I locked the door, night was falling, and we took each other by the hand.

HAPPY MEAL

I love this girl. I want to make her happy. I'd like to take her out to lunch. A big French brasserie with mirrors and proper tablecloths. So I can sit next to her, gaze at her profile, look at the people all around us and let everything get cold. I love her.

"Okay," she says, "but we're going to McDonald's."

She doesn't give me the time to protest.

"It's been ages," she adds, putting her book down by her side, "seems like forever . . . "

She's exaggerating. It was less than two months ago, I counted. I know how to count, but I'm resigned. The young lady likes her nuggets and barbecue sauce: what am I supposed to do?

If we're together long enough, I'll teach her about other things.

About grand veneur sauce, Pomerol wines, and crêpes Suzette, for example. If we're together long enough, I'll teach her that waiters at the big brasseries are not allowed to touch our napkins, and that they slide them onto the table by raising their presentation napkin slightly. That ought to astonish her. There are so many things I want to show her. So, so many things. But I say nothing while I watch her buttoning up her pretty coat.

I know what girls are like when it comes to the future: they make promises, and that's it. I'd rather take her to that crap fast food place and make her happy one day at a time. The crêpes Suzette can wait.

In the street I compliment her on her shoes. She takes offense:

"Don't tell me you never noticed them, I've had them since Christmas!"

I mumble something, she smiles at me, so I compliment her on her socks and she tells me I'm being dumb. As if I didn't already know.

We go through the door and I instantly feel nauseous. From one time to the next I forget how much I hate McDonald's. That smell . . . that smell of frying fat, ugliness, cruelty to animals, and vulgarity combined. Why do the female employees allow themselves to get so ugly? Why do they wear that pointless sun visor? Why do people stand in line so passively? Why do they play that elevator music? Where is the elevator? I stamp my feet with impatience. The customers ahead of us have no manners. The young women are vulgar and the young men have an empty stare. I have a hard enough time with humanity as it is: I shouldn't come to this sort of place.

I stand straight and stare at a point far ahead of me, as far away as possible: the price of the Maxi Best Of menus and the chemical composition of the Very Parfait posted above the counter. "Maxi Best Of." "Very Parfait." How can anyone make words sounds so ridiculous? I'm getting depressed. She can tell, she senses these things. She takes my hand and gives it a gentle squeeze. She doesn't look at me. I feel better. Her little finger is stroking my palm and my fortune line is overlapping my love line.

She changes her mind several times. For dessert she hesitates between a milkshake and a caramel sundae. She wrinkles her cute little nose and twirls a strand of hair with her finger. The waitress is tired and I feel emotional. I carry both our trays. She turns to me and says,

"I suppose you would rather sit all the way at the back?"

I shrug.

"You would. You like it better there. I know you do."

She clears the way for me. People who are sitting in the way scrape their chairs as she goes by. Faces turn. She doesn't see them. The impalpable disdain of the young lady who knows she is beautiful. She is looking for a little niche where the two of us will be comfortable. She finds a spot, smiles at me again, and I close my eyes in agreement. I put our pittance down on a table smeared with squirts of ketchup and streaks of grease. She slowly unwinds her scarf and wiggles her head three times before she reveals her graceful neck. I go on standing there like a big ninny.

"What are you waiting for?" she asks.

"I'm looking at you."

"You can look at me later. It's going to get cold."

"You're right."

"I'm always right."

"No, my love. Not always."

A little grimace.

I stretch my legs out into the aisle. I don't know where to begin. I already want to leave. There's nothing I like about these little parcels. A boy with a nose-ring is joined by two other loudmouths. I fold my legs under the table to let this strange herd go by.

I have a moment's doubt. What am I doing here? With my vast love and my tweed jacket? I feel a ridiculous urge to go and get a knife and fork.

She is worried:

"Is something wrong?"

"No, no. Everything's fine."

"Then eat!"

I do as she says. She delicately opens her box of nuggets as if it were a jewelry box. I look at her nails. A bluish polish.

Dragonfly wing polish. I'm telling you, I don't know anything about nail polish colors, but as it happens she also has two little dragonflies in her hair. Tiny barrettes that just barely hold a few blonde strands in place. I feel a surge of emotion. I know, I'm repeating myself, but I cannot help but wonder: was it for my sake, as she thought about our lunch together, that she painted her nails this morning?

I picture her in her bathroom, concentrating, and already dreaming of her caramel sundae. And of me at the same time. Oh yes. Of me. Inevitably.

She dips her pieces of defrosted chicken into their plastic sauce.

She's relishing it.

"You really like that?"

"I love it."

"But why?"

A triumphant smile.

"Because it's good!"

She's implying that I'm an old-fashioned killjoy, I can see it in her eyes. But at least she shows it tenderly.

Pray God it lasts, this tenderness. Pray God it lasts.

I join in. I chew and swallow, keeping time with her. She doesn't say a lot. I'm used to that. She never says much when I take her out to lunch. She's far too busy looking at the tables around her. People fascinate her. Even that weirdo at the next table wiping his mouth and blowing his nose in the same napkin is more interesting to her than I am.

And while she's looking at him, I take a moment to stare at her, undisturbed.

What do I like best about her?

Top of the list, I would say her eyebrows. She has lovely eyebrows. Very well drawn. The Great Architect must have been inspired that day. He probably used a sable brush and his hand did not tremble. Number two, her earlobes. Perfect. Her ears are not pierced. I hope she will never succumb to that ludicrous temptation. I will stop her. Number three, something that is very tricky to describe. For number three, I love her nose or, more precisely, her nostrils. The soft little round backs of those two tiny shells. Those pale pink shells, almost white, like the ones we have been looking for every summer since we met and which the kids on the beach call cowries. As for number four . . .

But the spell has been broken already: she could tell I was looking at her, and she simpers as she nibbles on her drinking straw. I look away. I hunt for my phone, patting my pockets.

"You put it in my bag."

"Thank you."

"What would you do without me, huh?"

"Nothing."

I smile at her and reach for a handful of cold fries.

"I would do nothing," I continue, "but I wouldn't have to go to McDonald's on a Saturday afternoon."

She didn't hear me. She has started on her sundae. With the tip of her spoon she starts by eating the chopped peanuts, then proceeds conscientiously along each swirl of caramel.

Then she pushes her tray back.

"Aren't you going to finish it?"

"No. I don't actually like sundaes. I just like the peanut bits and the caramel. The ice cream makes me feel sick."

"You want me to ask them to put some more on?"

"Some more what?"

"Some more peanuts and caramel."

"They'll never do it."

"Why not?"

"I just know they won't. They won't want to."

"Let me try."

I get up, holding her little cup of ice cream, and head toward the cash registers. I wink at her. She looks at me, amused. My heart is in my boots. I'm a valiant knight who is carrying his princess's colors to a faraway, hostile land.

In hushed tones I ask the woman for another sundae. It's easier that way. I'm a valiant knight who has some experience.

Off she goes again, painstakingly picking at her dessert. I like her gourmandise. I like her manners.

So graceful.

How is this possible?

I think about what to do next. Where shall I take her? What am I going to do with her? Will she give me her hand when we're back out in the street? Will she pick up her charming chirruping where she left it when we came in? What was she talking about, anyway? I think it was about Easter weekend. Where were we going for Easter? Good lord, my dear, I don't even know myself. I can try to make you happy from one day to the next, but ask me what we'll be doing two months from now, that's going a bit far. I'll have to find another topic of conversation, in addition to a place to go for a walk.

Valiant, experienced, and inspired.

Maybe the booksellers . . . the booksellers are just a pretext for strolling along the Seine. She will let out a sigh. "Again? Those old books, *again*?" No, she won't sigh. She likes to please me, too. And besides, she will give me her hand, I know she will. She has always given me her hand.

She folds her napkin before wiping her mouth. As she gets up, she smoothes her skirt and tugs on the sleeves of her cardigan. She picks up her bag and her glance indicates where I have to leave our trays.

I hold the door for her. The cold air is a shock. She ties her scarf again then with a confident gesture frees her hair from under her coat collar. She turns to thank me:

"That was delicious."

It was delicious.

We head down the rue Dauphine, the wind is blowing, I put my arm around her shoulder and hold her close.

How I love this girl. My little girl, my daughter. Her name is Adèle and she's not even six years old.

HIT POINTS

This morning, just before ten, I felt my phone vibrate in my shirt pocket. It went on buzzing but I didn't pay any attention because I was crouching down by a wall, examining the progression of a crack.

With my knee on my hard hat, I was trying to understand why a brand-new residential apartment complex was doomed never to be inhabited.

I had been appointed as an assessor by the insurance company representing the architects who had designed it, and I was waiting for my assistant to finish reading the numbers on the gauges we had installed all along that same crack four months earlier.

I won't go into the details now because it would be far too technical, but the situation was tense. Our agency had been working on this case for over two years, and a huge amount of money was at stake. A massive amount of money, the reputation of three architects, two surveyors, one property developer, one earthwork contractor, one building contractor, one foreman, two consulting engineers, and one deputy mayor.

We had to determine the "tendency of the disorder," as we say, modestly, in our jargon, and depending on which one of these three words was used in my future report—"displacement," "slippage," or "inclination" (and all their corollaries)—a decision would be made regarding not the amount—a subtle factor that was not my responsibility—but the names of the issuer and recipient of the future invoice.

So it's no wonder that I was not alone that morning at the bedside of a building that had scarcely risen from the ground but was already dying, and that my telephone could go on ringing in the void.

Which it did, and then it started again, as a matter of fact. Two minutes later. Annoyed, I put my hand inside my jacket. No sooner had I gagged the thing than my assistant François's phone took over. It went on ringing for a long while, six or seven times maybe, and twice over, but François was otherwise engaged, hanging in a basket thirty feet above the ground, so the stubborn ass trying to reach him eventually gave up.

I was thinking, sighing, running my hand over that damned crack, the third to appear on that facade since the beginning of our investigation, and I was touching it lightly with my fingertips the way I would have touched a human wound. With a similar sensation of impotence and in a similar vaguely Christlike delirium.

Wall, close thy gap.

I hated this moment in my life. I could tell the job was too much for me, for us, my partner and me, too heavy with consequence, too difficult and, above all, too risky. Regardless of the tenor of my report, and even if the fallout of this case, in the long run, would depend on grandstanding among lawyers, where the most alarming cracks, structures, and foundations always come to an amicable financial agreement, I knew that the mere fact of voicing my opinion, our opinion, would earn us the opprobrium of an entire sector of our branch of the profession.

If the architects were cleared, we would lose the clientele of the incriminated developer and contractor, and if the architects were held responsible, we wouldn't be paid for months (even years) and we would lose something even more precious than any pecuniary comfort: trust.

Trust in them, trust in us, and, by extension, trust in our profession. Because if they turned out to be guilty, it would be the proof that they'd been lying to us all along.

We hesitated a long time before we accepted this mission, and if we took it on it was because we had respect for these people. These people and their work. We went ahead with it, with everything it implied in the way of risk (we had to invest in extremely expensive equipment) because we always believed in their good faith.

Any proof we'd been mistaken would also, in and of itself, for my associate and me at any rate, be a terrible disorder.

It just so happened that that morning, and for the first time since we had begun this assessment work, I was beginning to have my doubts. Pointless to explain why, just then—that would be, I'll say it again, far too technical, but I was abnormally nervous. There were two or three details that were bugging me, and an insidious little thought was beginning to gnaw away at me. Just like those termites or capricorn beetles we went after from one assessment to the next: a *xylophagous* little thought.

For the first time since the start of our investigation and in all the hundreds of hours I'd spent on the case, I could sense something really nasty beginning to get at me from inside: had the architects really told us the whole truth?

(This is a long preamble, but it seems important, in light of the ensuing events to be related here. Everything is in the foundations. My profession has taught me that.)

I had reached this point in my ruminations when one of those same architects came up to me with his telephone.

"Your wife."

Before I even heard her voice I understood that she was the one who had been trying to reach me earlier, and before I even heard what she had to say I was imagining the worst.

It is impossible to exaggerate the incredible speed with which the cogs in one's brain turn, click, engage, and become alarmed. Before I'd even said those two little syllables, hel-lo, a succession of mental images, each one more morbid than the one before, had time to unreel before my eyes, and as I was still reaching for the phone I was convinced that something dreadful had happened.

Horrible thousandths of a second. Horrible seismic tremors. Crack, flaw, breach, fissure, however you want to put it, in that moment your heart weakens once and for all.

"The school," she said, breathlessly, "Valentin's school. They called me. There's a problem. You have to go there."

"What sort of problem?"

"I don't know. They wouldn't say over the phone. They want us to go there."

"But has something happened to him?"

"No, he did something."

"Something serious?"

And as I was asking her, I felt my heart start beating again. If nothing had happened to the boy, then the rest had to be insignificant. The rest no longer existed and I went back to inspecting my wall.

(And it is only tonight, as I write, "I went back to inspecting my wall," that I realize how this assessment job has driven me half-insane.)

"It must be, otherwise they wouldn't have summoned us like this. Pierre, you have to go."

"Now? No. I can't. I'm at the Pasteur site and I can't just leave, now. We're waiting for the results—"

"Look," she interrupted, "for two years you've been making our lives hell with that site, I know it's tough and I've never reproached you about anything, but now I need you. I have appointments up to my ears, I can't just cancel them all, and besides, you're closer. You have to go."

Okay. I won't spell out all the details because, once again, it would be too technical, but I know my wife well enough to know that when she speaks to me in that tone of voice, I have to respond.

"Okay. I'll go."

"Keep me posted, okay?"

She seemed really worried.

She seemed so worried that it spread to me like a contagion, and I simply called out to everyone that my little boy had a problem and I'd be back as soon as I could. I felt the cruel wind of incomprehension blow through the assembly. But no one dared say a thing. A child, even for sharks like them, was still a bit more precious than a sack of cement.

From up in his basket François gave me a reassuring sign. A sign that said, more or less: Don't worry. I've got my eye on them. A magnificent sign, given the circumstances. Magnificent.

* * *

The principal herself came out to the gate of the Victor Hugo Elementary School, which our three boys attended. She didn't greet me, didn't smile, didn't hold out her hand. She said nothing other than, "Come with me."

I knew her. We always exchanged a few words during school festivities, parent-teacher conferences, or class outings, and I had even done some work for her for free a few years ago when the town hall was expanding the cafeteria. (The "school restaurant," as they refer to it now.) Everything had gone well, and I was under the impression that our relations were in good standing.

As we were walking past the new building, I asked her whether everything was fine, where it was concerned, and she didn't answer. Or didn't hear. Her gait was rapid, her fists were clenched, and her face was unfriendly.

Sensing such hostility on her part took me back forty years. I suddenly felt like the sheepish little boy walking silently behind the principal, wondering what his punishment would be, whether his parents would be notified. A very unpleasant sensation, believe me.

Very unpleasant and very odd.

Very unpleasant as far as I was concerned, because it was more than a sensation, it was a memory—I'd been a troublesome pupil, the little boy who was held by the ear and marched across the schoolyard as if to the gallows; but it was odd, too, in the case of my son Valentin, because he was as gentle and kind as they come.

What on earth had he done?

For the second time that morning I was confronted with a mystery that was beyond me. What design flaw in the mind of my six-year-old son had caused his little world, or that of his school in any case, to show forewarnings of *displacement*, *slippage*, or *inclination*?

Nothing would have surprised me, coming from his brothers, but him? He had always been deeply respectful of his teachers, he kept his notebooks perfectly tidy, shared his toys, and when he was at my in-laws' on vacation, he would rather run the length of their swimming pool from morning to night to fish out any drowning insects than actually swim in it himself: this boy, punished?

My gift child, as I often call him, because that's what he is, literally. Our two eldest were already getting big, Thomas was eight and Gabriel was six, and one year when their mother

Juliette asked me what I would like for Christmas I said, a baby. We just missed Christmas but, since he was born in mid-February, we called him Valentin.

He was Valentin, and he was a marvel.

How could my gift child, barely six years old, have put the principal of his school in such a state? It was a complete enigma.

Her office was on the second floor of the main building. She went in first and motioned to me to follow, never looking at me.

I followed.

"Close the door behind you," she ordered.

If I'd had a voltage tester in my hand, I think the thing would have electrocuted me. This wasn't a meeting, this was an electromagnetic field.

In the room there was a man with a somber expression who responded to my greeting with a tiny nod, a woman so full of outrage that she didn't have the breath to respond, a little boy in a wheelchair, their son no doubt, who did not look up at me, absorbed as he was in scratching an imaginary spot on the knee of his trouser leg, and, all alone, facing them, standing by the window, my son Valentin.

He was backlit and staring at his feet.

"Valentin will explain to you why I sent for you so urgently this morning, along with Maxime's parents," announced the principal, turning to my son.

No answer.

"Valentin," she repeated, "at least find the courage to tell your father what you did."

Maxime's dad was looking sternly at my son, Maxime's mom was shaking her head indignantly and fiddling with her car keys, Maxime was looking out the window, and Valentin was still staring at his feet.

"Valentin," I said softly, "tell me what you did."

No answer.

"Valentin, look at me."

The boy obeyed, and I found myself looking at a child I'd never seen. If you could even call him a child; this was a wall. His face was a wall and the wall was far more solid than the ones I'd been so focused on not half an hour earlier. A great stone wall, with two big, fair eyes for arrow slits. A fortress.

Of course, I couldn't let anything show, but inside I was smiling. He was so cute, with his little air of a young soldier about to be court-martialed. No, he wasn't cute, he was handsome.

So handsome, calm, and pale . . . A statue. Of white marble.

"Valentin," said the principal again, "don't make me have to tell them myself, please."

Maxime's mom let out a little hiccup and her hiccup annoyed me. What was going on, anyway? Their son was alive, by the look of it, and surely it wasn't my son who had put him in his wheelchair! I was about to interrupt, to give voice to my irritation, when my little boy resolved to confess—and I can never thank him enough for that—and thereby saved me from ridicule before this gathering full of sorrow and fury.

"I punctured the tire on Maxime's wheelchair . . . " he murmured.

"Precisely!" retorted the principal, in a smug tone. "You punctured the tire on your little classmate's wheelchair, using the tip of your compass. That is precisely what you did. Are you proud of yourself?"

No answer.

No answer on the part of a six-year-old boy hitherto known for his kindness was tantamount to acquiescing, and if he was taking responsibility for his deed in this way, the least anyone could do was conduct a little investigation.

Mind you, I'm not saying I was already prepared to cover

for him or forgive the sins of my offspring, but it was my profession to conduct investigations in order to determine the responsibility of the parties involved in a dispute, and I would insist on a preliminary assessment before determining the causes of a claim.

I wasn't protecting my son, I was enforcing the law. And that morning I was all the more scrupulous about it, given that I was having such a fussy time with the truth.

For months I'd been stressed, mistreated, shoved this way and that by people who were playing cat and mouse with reality, and when it came down to it I was really in need of the utmost clarity.

"Are you proud of yourself?" she asked him again.

No answer.

The principal turned to Maxime's parents, raising her arms in a sign of exasperation.

Relieved that Valentin had confessed, and reassured by the unfailing support of Authority, Maxime's dad sat up straighter and his mom put away her keys.

The tension fell a few thousand volts and you could tell that now it was time to move on to more serious things, namely: the punishment. What would be a fitting sentence for such a cowardly act? For you must agree, ladies and gentlemen of the jury, that there is nothing worse on earth than attacking a poor, defenseless, disabled child, now is there?

Yes, I could feel the tension abating and I did not like the nature of this easing. I didn't like it because it was covering the cracks a bit too quickly. I knew my son, I knew what he was made of, his foundations, and it was not like him to commit such an act without good reason.

"Why did you do it?" I asked, flashing him an invisible smile, hidden in my eyebrows above my big-mean-but-only-pretend-mean eyes.

No answer.

I was disconcerted. I knew my boy must have seen my real-pretend-angry-dad grimace, so why didn't he stop his own scowl? Why didn't he trust me?

"You don't want to tell me?"

He shook his head.

"Why don't you want to tell me?"

No answer.

"He doesn't want to tell you because he's ashamed!" asserted Maxime's mom.

"Are you ashamed?" I repeated gently, still holding his gaze.

No answer.

"Okay, look . . . " sighed the principal, "I don't want to keep you any longer over such a regrettable incident. We have the facts, and the facts are unforgiveable. If Valentin won't speak, too bad. He will be punished, and that will give him time to think about his behavior."

Sighs of relief in the courtroom.

I did not take my eyes off my son. I wanted to understand.

"Go back to class," she ordered.

As he was heading to the door, I called out, "Valentin, is it that you *don't want* to tell me or that you *can't* tell me?"

He froze. No answer.

"You can't tell me?"

No answer.

"You can't tell me because it's a secret?"

And then, because he nodded his head for the first time, the gentle shaking of his neck allowed two huge teardrops lodged in his eyelashes to escape at last and slide down his cheeks.

Oh . . . I melted with tenderness. I wanted so badly, in that moment, to kneel before him and hug him tight. Hug him tight and whisper in his ear, "It's fine, kiddo, it's fine. You have a secret to keep and you have to keep it, even when you're threatened. You know I'm proud of you. I don't know why you did this, but I know you have your reasons and that's enough for me. I know who you are. I trust you."

Of course, I didn't move. Not out of a fear of displeasing the principal or protecting my son's modesty, but out of respect for Maxime's parents. Out of respect for the kind of suffering that had nothing to do with this stupid business about a tire. Out of respect for these people who only wished they, too, could kneel at their son's feet, and hold him to their hearts.

I didn't move, but some professional reflex got the better of me once again. In that very moment it became perfectly clear that it was time for them, for me, for Valentin, Maxime, and the entire academic institution as represented here by the principal, to proceed with an umpteenth expert's report.

Yes, it was my duty to "define the conservational measures necessary to ensure the safety of the work, or to avoid any aggravation of disorder," so I placed a hand on my son's shoulder to stop him leaving the room. Thus, holding him against my legs, I swung around so that we were both facing Maxime's parents.

I looked at them and said:

"Look. I am not defending my son. What he did was really not very smart. And what's more, he is going to help me fix what he's done because I have a tire patch kit in the trunk of the car and I am going to take this opportunity to show him, to show both of them," I said, turning to Maxime, "how to repair an inner tube. It's always a good thing to know and it might come in useful in life. So that's one thing, let's move on. This incident with the wheelchair is really of no great importance. However, what is important, and I know that what I am about to say may seem shocking to you, but I really believe this, is that Valentin behaved well toward your son this morning. He behaved well because he did not treat him any differently from any other kid. And do you know why? I imagine it's because he does not see any difference between himself and Maxime. To Valentin, Maxime is neither weak nor vulnerable. He's just a boy like all the others and who must, therefore, be subjected to the same tough laws of the playground as all the other kids. There was no discrimination on his part, not even any *positive* discrimination, as we say, we adults who are always trying to discriminate for and against everything. No, he treated him as an equal. For reasons we don't understand, and we can't understand because children's secrets are sacred, Valentin felt obliged to go after your son. If he could have, he would have beaten him up, or tripped him, or punched him in the shoulder or who knows what else, but since he couldn't, he took it out on his wheelchair. Fair enough. It was only fair and I would even go so far as to say it was healthy. Our children see themselves as being on an equal footing and it is wrong of us"—here I turned to face the principal—"it is wrong of us to make a huge deal out of such a banal event. If Valentin had come to blows with some other kid in the schoolyard," I asked her, "would you have summoned the parents as if it were some state of emergency? No. Of course not. Whichever adult was there to keep an eye on things would have separated them and that would have been the end of it. Well, this is the same. The equivalent of tripping him, no more, no less."

Then, turning back to Maxime's parents:

"I'll say it again, I'm not excusing my son, I'm not excusing him and I also want him to be punished, but I maintain that far from humiliating your son, by puncturing his tire he honored him."

As I was in a hurry to get back to work, and they were all getting on my nerves, these old adults who just don't understand children, because they've already forgotten every last

THE CRACKS IN OUR ARMOR · 121

thing about their own childhood, I didn't wait for any of them to comment on my long tirade and I went on with the task of shoring things up.

"Tell me," I said to the principal, "where can I find a big bowl of water? And you, Valentin, push this deflated chair, slowly, and follow me out to the parking lot."

While the others were coming to their senses, still somewhat stunned by my assessment of conditions in the field, I lifted little Maxime up by the armpits to carry him out to my object lesson.

He wasn't heavy, I picked him up as if it were nothing, and I was the one, at that particular moment, yes, I was by far the most stunned of the four adults there in the room.

In that moment I was overcome by a dizziness of a sort I'd never felt in my entire life. It almost caused me to falter.

No, wait, careful there, "dizziness" is not the right word. When I picked that little six-year-old boy up, it wasn't dizziness I felt, but such immense sorrow that the impact of it almost made me lose my balance.

Why such a slippage when not even a minute earlier I stood there as upright in my boots as in my convictions, lecturing my little crowd like some lawyer for the defense?

Because.

Because I am the father of three boys. Because for nearly fifteen years I have been taking children in my arms, hundreds of times. Hundreds and hundreds of times.

Because—and every adult who has often made this gesture will understand—if there is one thing that is gentle and reassuring and makes you feel safe, yes, that's precisely it, safe (and God knows I am familiar with all the ways to reinforce structural walls so they'll be safe), as safe in your soul as in your body when you're taking a child in your arms, well, it has to be the "koala" instinct.

The moment you pick up a child, or any young mammal in a similar manner, I suppose, they will raise their legs and curl them around your waist. It's instinctive. No sooner do you hold out your arms than their natural intelligence will tell them to prop themselves against you, and they will not seem nearly as heavy.

Wonderful nature.

Wonderful nature, but so incoherent, granting to one what it withholds from another: little Maxime with his dead legs weighed more than I do.

I didn't expect it.

I instantly stopped acting the resident idiot know-it-all specialist who spouts his theories left, right, and center, I reached for the boy's legs to tuck them up around my center of gravity, said goodbye to the principal, and humbly enjoined his parents to follow me out to the parking lot.

If we were going to stand there patching tires, might as well patch them all together, it would be more fun.

* * *

And it was more fun. Maxime's dad was named Arnaud and his mom, Sandrine. They weren't angry, they were tired.

Since I didn't want to let go of their son's warm arms—I suppose it was both an unconscious desire to expiate my earlier irritation and my sermon, and the presence on this earth of my three sound, robust children—it was Sandrine who found a container with some water and Arnaud who removed the tire. He also took over the task of showing the boys how to find the hole in the inner tube by watching the little bubbles rising, and how important it was to sand and clean the rubber carefully before applying the patch.

In the meanwhile I acted as crane, drag, forklift, and articulated boom lift for one very inquisitive little boy.

A role that enchanted me. I hadn't felt that useful on a construction site in ages.

I had no time to take Arnaud and Sandrine up on their suggestion we go for a coffee, because my measurements were waiting, but we parted in peace and reinflated, so to speak, while Maxime and Valentin went back to work.

Maxime pushed his wheels on his own and Valentin walked by his side.

I was about to call out, "Push him, come on!" then thought better of it.

Show some logic, Mr. Assessor Man, show some logic.

* * *

"183 millimeters for the G1, 79 for the G2, 51 universal, and 12 along the axis," announced François the minute I got off the phone, and hadn't even had time to put it (and all of Juliette's anxiety) back in my pocket.

As I remained silent, he added:

"Are you surprised?"

The hatchback of his company car was wide open and, comfortably seated on a metal drum, he was typing on his laptop in the trunk before him.

"You're not surprised?" he said, surprised, while I was again looking at the northern facades of the Résidence des Ormes.

This magnificent housing project, with fifty-nine apartments, empty, but available for immediate occupation—or so proclaimed the billboard there in front of me, in letters twelve feet high by nine feet wide—in July of the previous year.

"It, uh—" I murmured.

"What?"

He motioned to me that he couldn't hear because of his hard hat.

"How much longer do you need?"

"I'm almost done."

"Finish after. Let's go get lunch. We're not in such a rush now."

* * *

To be honest, I never tried to uncover Valentin's secret, and I probably never would have, were it not for Léo, Thomas's best friend, who had a little sister who was also six years old.

This little sister was named Amélie and this Amélie was a real chatterbox.

She had told her brother about "the really naughty thing Valentin did"—a really naughty thing that had been the talk of the entire school, the only subject of conversation among all the pupils and all the adults who had been there that day, and it went without saying that Valentin's misdemeanor would go down in the annals of that little schoolyard for centuries to come. Amélie was a chatterbox so that very evening, when we were all having supper, this is what Juliette and I overheard:

Gabriel: Hey, Vava.

Valentin: What?

Gabriel: Is it true you punctured the tire on the wheelchair of some dude in your class today?

Valentin: Yes.

The two older boys burst out laughing.

Thomas: You thought you were playing Mille Bornes or something?

More snickers.

Gabriel: What'd'you do it with, a thumbtack?

Valentin: No.

Thomas: A nail?

Valentin: No.

Gabriel: What, then?

Valentin: My compass.

Real laughter.

Thomas: Why? What'd he do to you?

(And I noticed, then, the wisdom of children: for a start, there was nothing respectable about wheelchairs per se, and secondly, in the schoolyard you never lash out at anyone without a good reason.)

No answer.

Gabriel: You don't want to say?

No answer.

Thomas: Did he insult you?

No answer.

Gabriel: Did he steal your pencil case, the moron?

Valentin (shocked): He's not a moron. Besides, he has all the *Ariol* comics and all the *Kid Paddles*.

Gabriel: No way. Well then, what'd he do to you?

No answer, and our little Valentin was once again on the verge of tears.

The big boys adored their little brother. To them, too, he was a gift, and they were upset to see him like that, all sad and on the brink.

Gabriel: Vava, tell us right now what he did, otherwise tomorrow we'll go and ask him ourselves.

Valentin (who felt a tremor from head to foot at such a threat): I . . . I can't . . . can't tell you, (sobbing) because Mommy will scold me.

Juliette (amused, moved) (but above all moved): No, go ahead. You can say. I promise I won't scold you.

Gabriel (triumphant): Oh, I know! I know what it is! Something to do with the Pokémon cards!

Valentin (devastated): Yee . . . ees.

This business with the Pokémon cards had become a very sensitive issue at home, because Valentin (introduced, infected, catechized, converted, indoctrinated, and guided by his brothers) was crazy about them, and he'd already been punished several times because of them. His mother had therefore strictly forbidden him from taking them to school where, in any event, they were already strictly forbidden. (And suddenly I understood why he had remained so stoic in the presence of the principal, preferring to be punished for cowardice rather than for disobedience.)

In the face of such sorrow and moral rectitude, I finally allowed myself to do what I had sternly refrained from doing much earlier that day: I got up and walked around the table to give my son a huge hug.

He was in my arms, with his smell of chalk, innocence, fatigue, chamomile shampoo, and childish despair. He was in my arms with his wet nose and his pudgy koala paws clinging to my hips, and from his perch on his daddy he hiccupped over at his brothers:

"He . . . he . . . lied. He made me tr-trade a su-super rare card for a . . . a stupid one . . . He . . . he made me believe that . . . that it was a . . . Legen-Legendary . . . "

"Which one did you trade?" asked Gabriel imperturbably.

"My Heracross EX, with 170 aitchpees."

"Are you crazy?" exclaimed Thomas, "you never trade that one, you should know that!"

"Which one did he give you in exchange?" asked Gabriel.

"Wigglytuff."

Silence.

The two older boys were gobsmacked. After a few seconds of utter astonishment, Thomas repeated, incredulously:

"Wigglytuff? That rotten little Wigglytuff with 120 aitchpees?"

"Ye-yees," sobbed Valentin, ever harder.

"But . . . But . . . " Gabriel was breathless with indignation.

"All you have to do is look at Wigglytuff to know he's useless. He's all pink and silly. Like some stuffed animal for girls."

"Yes, but . . . but Maxime told me that . . . that he was a Le . . . Le . . . Legendary Pokémon."

Thomas and Gabriel were in shock. To swap a Heracross EX for a Wigglytuff was already disgraceful enough, but to carry off such a heist by maintaining that Wigglytuff was a Legendary Pokémon: well, that was really the most rock-bottom down-dirty mean-and-nasty trick of any infamy ever committed on a playground. I looked at their crushed expressions—like fall guys whose wives had cheated on them to boot—and couldn't help but roar with laughter. Two petty Mafiosi taken for a ride by one six-and-a-half-year-old Joe Pesci.

After a minute of tomblike silence, where nothing could be heard but the clatter of cutlery, Thomas said, as if ringing the death knell:

"You were too nice, Valentin. You were way too nice. You should have punctured *both* his tires, the big fat liar . . . "

* * *

After tucking him in bed, a while ago, I asked him:

"Tell me, then, what does it mean, aitchpees?"

"Hit points."

"Oh . . . I see."

"The more HPs your Pokémon has," he added, taking a card out from under his mattress to show me the number in the upper right-hand corner, "the stronger it is, you see?"

I knew that this wasn't really the right time, but I couldn't resist, and I added:

"Do you still have your Wigglytuff card?"

A shadow instantly went over his face.

"Yes," he moaned, "but it's stupid."

"You want to trade it with me?" I asked him, switching off his bedside lamp.

"Oh, no . . . I won't trade it, I'll give it to you. It's too stupid. Why do you want it?"

"I want to keep it as a souvenir."

"A souvenir of what?" he asked, with a yawn.

* * *

Valentin drifted off before he could hear my reply, and it's a good thing he did, because I didn't even know it myself.

What could I have said?

A souvenir of you. Of me. Of your brothers and your mom. A souvenir of this day.

When I find out the answers, I write up reports.

I spend my life writing reports, that's how I make my living.

Now it's almost three o'clock in the morning, the whole house is asleep, I'm still sitting at the kitchen table, and I've just finished my first ever expert's report without a conclusion.

I just wanted to make a record of what I went through today.

My family, my job, my worries, what still surprises me and what no longer surprises me, my naiveté, my privileges, my good fortune . . .

My foundations.

My hit points.

THE FOOT SOLDIER

Where are you, Louis?
Where are you, what have they done with you?
Have they burned you? Buried you? Can we still come and see you?
And if so, where? Where, exactly?
In Paris? In the provinces?

Where are you and how should I *imagine* you now?
Under a slab? Deep inside a tomb? In an urn?
Dressed, recumbent, wearing makeup and nearly decomposed,
or in ashes?
Or scattered, dispersed, spread
lost
Louis.
You were so handsome . . .

What have they done with you?

What have they done with you and who are they, anyway?
Who are these people you never spoke about?
Did you have a family?
Of course you did. Every day I go down a boulevard that bears your name. I have forgotten what your connection was with the family of that victorious Marshal of the Empire, but you did have a family, of course you did.

What sort of family?
Who are they? What are they worth?
Did you love them? Did they love you? Did they respect your last wishes?

What were your last wishes, Louis?

shit, Louis,
shit
you piss me off

Seoul, ten o'clock at night, I'm stationed in a hotel room on the forty-first floor of a tower that has just risen from the ground. I think I must be the first occupant. The workers who installed the carpet left their cutter here and the sides of the shower stall are still covered with protective film.

I arrived here from Toronto where for three days I had one interview after another, after two quick stops at production sites, one in Warsaw and the other in the outskirts of Vilnius. I've accumulated so many hours of jet lag in one direction and then the other that my biological clock no longer has a grip on any sort of reality. I'm holding on is all, holding on.

While hunting for a memo for an agent from Tao Tanglin, with whom I'm supposed to have breakfast tomorrow, I came by chance upon this file, *Untitled* 1, in the depths of my computer. I had no memory of writing those words and I even find it hard to believe I was their author.

I had just opened your gift. I was unhappy. I had been drinking.

Like a fish.

Louis.
I'm back.
Several months have gone by and here I am again today, calmer and not as coarse, but I'm still wondering the same things, you know . . .

I'm wondering the same things and I still come to the same conclusion: I miss you, my friend.

I miss you so much.

I would never have imagined it was possible to miss you this much. It's not an expression, I'm not saying "I miss you" the way I might come and complain to you about a lack of sleep, or sunlight, or courage, or time; I'm telling you this as if some part of myself had gone missing. The best part, perhaps. The only serene part, the kindest. The most watchful.

You are watching over me now the way you watched over me two years ago.

Two years, Louis, two years.

How can that be?

To have instilled so much life in so few days . . .

Phantom limb, pseudohallucination, PATHOL. *noun: Illusory and occasionally painful perception of an amputated limb. Pain revived by stress, anxiety, and meteorological changes.*

That's what I feel when I think about you. Ridiculous, isn't it?

Ridiculous. You were not only my compass, now it seems you'd become my barometer.

The slightest thing goes wrong, the least little oscillation, and I pat myself and search my body for proof of your absence.

I keep looking for you, Louis. Your death is like a wedge someone's rammed into my skull, and the slightest doubt, wham, a sledgehammer drives it in.

Wham.

I'll end up split in two.

What nonsense I'm writing.

Nonsense, for fear of speaking nonsense.

Two years.
If that.
Such a short time.
Such a short time, and how I regret those lost years.
We could have met much sooner, but we were discreet, you and I.
Discreet, distant, busy.
So busy.
So stupid, in other words.

I have a thousand more urgent problems to deal with, but I wish I could be with you.
I wish I could speak to you, see you, hear you.
I wish I could live through those years all over again.
It's the right time. I am, as I was saying, as lifeless as can be.

Louis . . .
Don't go anywhere.
I'm going to pour myself a glass of something and I'll be back.

* * *

You were a lawyer, I was running a company—I still run it—and we were neighbors who shared a landing and sometimes met by the elevator or in the hallway of that posh building in the 16th arrondissement where we shared the top floor.

We sometimes crossed paths, but scarcely exchanged anything more than a distracted, tired nod, we were so stubborn—stubborn asses, we were, determined to become beasts of burden, each of us bending beneath the weight of our importance and the huge files we were dumb enough to bring into the circle of our private space.

(I had started to write "home," "dumb enough to bring home," and then I thought better of it. Did I have a home? Did you have a home? I replaced it with "the circle of our private space," but that's even more grotesque. The circle of our private space. What bullshit. Why not the circle of greyhound racing or a private dining club while I'm at it?)

If we shared any intimacy, it was no more than that of two members of a private club, however exclusive. Not for a lack of opportunity, but we didn't have time, dear God. We didn't have time. Neither for hunting nor golf nor power, still less for anything private, that might verge on intimacy.

Intimacy . . .

The name of a magazine for hairdressers, don't you think?

As for the word "household," to me it was nothing more than a word used for tax purposes, to calculate the amount owing on my income, whereas for you . . .

Well, you lived alone, so I don't know.

Perhaps your evenings began not in a household, but in a lobby: theatres, operas, I imagine. Aisles, rows of seats, intermissions . . .

You went out a lot and . . . No. I really can't imagine. I don't know.

You were so secretive . . .

Often, when I was absent and had to catch an early-morning flight, I would run into you well before dawn. I noticed you, furtively, while my driver was hurrying to open the door to an overheated car, and there'd be this vision of you, so handsome, so pale, your hands in your pockets, your collar raised, your face blurred by the night and your nose half-buried in your scarf: that vision kept me company, for a long time.

My rides to the airport, my hours spent waiting, my battle plans, my troops to muster, my investors to reassure, my partners to win over, my moments of discouragement, their moments of discouragement, my doubts, and theirs, my reputation, my hardness, my fatigue, my headaches, my belly-aches, my ever-empty hotel rooms, my family always on voicemail, my never-ending jet lag, my combat medicine cabinet, my insomnia . . . all the trappings of the foot soldier to capitalism, an entire life of arm wrestling, fighting, passion, a life I chose, and fought for, a life I respect, even, but which exhausts me, and more than ever since your disappearance, my life, at those moments, depended solely on the memory of your elegant person.

Your person. You. Your freedom.

The memory of what I thought was freedom.

A woman of culture to whom I recently related our early-morning to-ings and fro-ings (I will tell you later the circumstances thereof), emphasizing the strange comfort they gave me, said mockingly:

"It sounds like Paul Morand calling out to Proust . . . "

I didn't react. I would rather be taken for a pedant than for an idiot.

There was no fooling her. She looked me straight in the eye for a long while, long enough to make me understand that I was, alas—no doubt about it, the proof being this long pause—a pedant of the worst kind: an idiot of a pedant and then, once this had been made perfectly clear, she moved her face closer to mine and added, in her lovely, deep voice:

"*Proust . . . What sort of soirée do you go to at night to come home with eyes so weary and lucid? And what fright, forbidden to us, did you have, to come back so indulgent and so kind?*"

Silence.

Her: Something like that, no?
I was silent.
Her: You won't say.

I wouldn't say, because . . .
Wham.

Your kindness, Louis.
Your kindness.

Night has fallen. Pollution and the lights of the city pay no heed to the fact, but I who am so close to you, in my ghost room almost two hundred meters from the ground, you cannot imagine how happy I am at the thought of spending the evening in your company.
Like the old days.

* * *

It's nearly midnight. I've just reread what I've written. 1535 words. Two hours spent scribbling and an entire minibar to produce 1535 words.
What a feat.
And 1535 words that don't mean a thing, on top of it. That understand nothing, express nothing, that simply echo: Shut up, Cailley-Ponthieu, shut up, go to bed. You're beating around the bush, dragging things out, acting the fine gentleman. You don't know how to write. You don't know how to express yourself. You're incapable of expressing the least little sentiment: incapable. You've never known how. It doesn't interest you.

Hard going, all that. Hard going, and pretentious.
"A wedge someone's rammed into my skull" and why not a

touch of Proust, while you're at it? Come on, come on. Straighten yourself up, please.

Take your sleeping pills, knock the beast out, collapse.

A wedge someone's rammed into my skull . . .

But nothing stays in your mind, old man. Nothing. And even less in your flesh. So you see, even there. Even, there, you say "flesh" in order not to say "heart," since the word makes you sick to your stomach. Heart, Cailley, heart. You know— that organ that is hard at work inside you. That pump. Motor.

Switch off the computer and go to bed. Go get some strength.

Go get some strength so you can go on pulling your wagons tomorrow morning.

Silence, up there, silence. I've been drinking, I am drinking, it will all work out. It has to. It has to come out. Like a blood-letting. I have to end things with you. I have to bury you, too. Whether I bury you or scatter you hardly matters, whatever you want, whatever you would have chosen, but I really have to put an end to this mourning which your discretion has deprived me of.

I have to bring you back to life one last time, so that at last I can say goodbye.

Say goodbye, let you rest in peace, and see if I can open your gift again now without crying like a baby.

* * *

I was saying, above, that we were restrained in our behavior toward each other, and only acknowledged each other with a courteous nod when we met in the common area of our building, but that's not altogether true. Our shoes, Louis, our shoes were more flexible than we were, and it was our shoes, if you recall, that took the first step.

We shared this one guilty weakness: shoes, and it wasn't just a way we could greet each other, it was also a furtive glance. No looking each other up and down, no, we would make the most of our stolen glances to verify that one thing, at least, in a world gone mad, was still as it should be: come rain, wind, or snow, the neighbor from across the hall would still be wearing shoes that had been styled and put together by a reputable house, and which were impeccably polished.

Now that was reassuring, was it not? Yes. So reassuring . . . a reassurance that is impossible to imagine for someone unacquainted with the early-morning pleasures of a heel slipping down the curve of a shoehorn, of a perfect pair of laces cinching up one's soul as firmly as one's leg, of the perforated trim on the toe adding a touch of fantasy beneath those suits that have none at all, of the double stitching which (in addition to being elegant) gives you the illusion it can never wear out, of a sheen that says more about you and your past life than you could ever possibly express on your own, or even of the wooden shoe trees that you cannot help but caress before you slip them into an exhausted shoe, and which immediately smooth out those creases on the uppers, on a day that has proven equally trying.

You and I both knew this and we were mutually grateful for the knowledge. For all that they were fleeting, our glances were no less appreciative. The knowing look of the connoisseur who recognizes his equal from his shoes, compounded with that of the reserved man awkwardly expressing his gratitude. The tiny smile hidden in the tiny nod, saying, more or less: Thank you, fellow believer, thank you. My blessings upon you.

The run-of-the-mill fellow wearing sneakers would no doubt maintain that I'm going overboard, but you, and a few others, will listen to me without batting an eyelash. A fine shoe, Louis, a nice pair, handsome Derbys, good-looking loafers, a shining buckle, an immaculate pair of bucks, box calf and leather saddle shoes, shoe trees made of alder wood, moiré calfskin suede, cordovan leather that squeaks when it's bent, a sheen like Japanese lacquer, a polish made of carnauba wax . . . Ah. Dear God. What could be finer?

Given my obligation to dress like a boss, you'll never see me shod in anything other than a pair of black Oxfords, with a straight or uniform toe, or in a pinch, an extreme pinch, on a Friday with no hassles in view, a perforated toe (what madness), but you, especially once I got to know you better, you have no idea, the thrill you could give me. Such a thrill. All our discussions. And animated debates. About this model over that one, this lack of taste rather than that one, a Hungarian bootmaker over a Viennese one, a Viennese one over a New Yorker; about an estimate, an impulse, a wise renunciation, a cobbler out in the back of beyond, the soft feel of an old rag, or the length of the hairs on a shoeshine brush. How many hours did they keep us enthralled, all these existential questions? How many hours? It seems to me we never spoke of anything else, just our shoes, our wonderful shoes—there to polish, to dream about, to get resoled—and that as we were talking we were exposing a great deal about ourselves to each other.

In a lifetime there are classmates, fellow students, army buddies, work colleagues, good friends, old friends, Holmes and Watson; and then there are encounters like ours. Which are all the more delightfully unexpected in that they are founded on nothing, no common past, encounters which, precisely because of that nothing in common you have in common, give free rein, under cover of something completely different (in this case, men's footwear), to the greatest moments of abandon.

Nothing is said; everything is understood.

Or, the invisible plunder of contraband friendships.

But I'm getting ahead of myself, getting ahead . . .

For the time being we are still in the entrance or the stairway, secretly spying on the tips of our shoes, whereas our first real encounter took place on our landing, and that evening I was standing there before you—reeling, in actual fact—in my shirtsleeves, barefoot.

* * *

It was a little over two years ago, at the end of December, when the days are so short, and the lack of light, along with the dread of year-end balance sheets, auditors, and family get-togethers, makes us all feel so vulnerable.

I've always worked like a dog, but even harder at that time of year. It was right in the middle of the oil crisis and I felt like that character in the Tex Avery cartoon who wears himself out trying to plug all the gushing leaks, running like a madman from one disaster to the next without ever managing to plug anything anywhere.

Business trips all over the place, endless meetings, and grim games of three-card Monte with talentless bankers, trying to patch things up. I won't go into the details because you already know them, Louis. I've told you everything. I told you long after the worst of the storm was over, and you forced me, without ever obliging me in any way, to relive it, out loud, in order to *understand.*

To understand what had happened, understand what I had lost, and above all—again, according to you—understand what I had gained.

(To be absolutely honest, I didn't really understand what you meant by that. It seems to me that, apart from our friendship, I didn't gain much from any of that painful business, but never mind, it hardly matters. You always said: "Be patient, be patient." Well look, how convenient, now you're dead, I have no family life left and I work even harder than I used to, so, as far as patience goes, I've got plenty.)

I was supposed to fly to Hamburg, I'd gotten up very early, and Ariane came into the bathroom while I was shaving.

She sat down behind me, on the edge of the bathtub.

Because she was wearing a pale nightgown, and the sleeves of the cardigan she'd borrowed from me were too long and hid her hands; because she hadn't buttoned it up but merely crossed it over her heart; and because she was hugging herself and gently swaying back and forth with her head down and her hair uncombed, I had a terrible vision: it was as if I were looking at the reflection of a madwoman. A lunatic in a straitjacket. But of course not; if she was holding herself like that it was to contain herself, to keep herself upright when at last she raised her head, and there was nothing neurotic about her gentle swaying, it was quite the contrary: she was gathering momentum.

(I often think back at how wrong I got it, Louis, and it seems that . . . that the ruin of my life is all there in that steamy mirror: I damage the people I love by reducing them to being even weaker than I am. There was nothing insane about Ariane that morning, she was merely silently gathering her strength to give herself courage. I never understand a thing. She was the one who was all-powerful; she was the one.)

I asked her if I'd woken her up and she replied that she hadn't slept a wink, and since I didn't react (had I even listened?) she added quietly that she was leaving me, that she was going to take the girls and move into an apartment two streets over, that I could go on seeing them whenever I liked, "Well . . . when you can," she amended, with a bitter grimace, but that this was it, the journey was over. She couldn't take it anymore, I was never there, she had met someone, a considerate man, who took care of his children and had custody every other week, she wasn't sure she was really in love, but she wanted to give that life a try, and see. See if it would be sweeter, lighter, simpler. She had made the decision as much for the girls' sake as for herself. Life here had become too difficult. I was constantly absent. Even when I was there. Especially when I was there. My stress had contaminated them all and she wanted Laure and Lucie to have a different kind of childhood. The concierge's husband would be coming to pick up her boxes that evening, she would take nothing besides her clothes and the girls', a few books, a few toys, and the key to the house in Calvi that I'd given her for her fortieth birthday. Divorce was out of the question for the moment, she would take Mako, the nanny-housekeeper, with her, but Mako would start her workday here, so it would be as if I were staying at a hotel, since I liked that so much, with my bed made and a clean bathroom every morning. She would go on using our joint account, but solely for the children, she had money and didn't want me to support her, she would always be accommodating where the girls were concerned, I could have them whenever I wanted and for as long as I wanted but for this vacation—which, I surely hadn't even realized, started that evening—everything was already planned: she would take them with her to spend two weeks in the sun.

I reached for a towel, dabbed my face, and when I finally turned around, she said,

"You know why I'm leaving you, Paul? I've leaving you because you didn't even nick yourself. I'm leaving you because you're the kind of man who can be told all this and come out of it without a single scratch."

I was speechless.

"You're a monster, Paul Cailley-Ponthieu. A kind monster, but a monster all the same."

I didn't respond. It was an old blade and I was already late.

I managed to stay on the phone all the way to the gate, but when I found out the flight was at least fifty minutes late (poor visibility), I hung up, switched the phone off, and collapsed in a seat, my legs like jelly.

A stranger roused me from my torpor.

"Monsieur? Are you all right?"

I apologized, pulled myself together, and left for Hamburg.

My driver dropped me off outside the house that same evening at around eight o'clock.

The front hall of the apartment was littered with cardboard boxes: *Shoes Me, Girls Summer Clothes, Lucie Stuffed Animals, Ariane Underwear.* Right.

I pulled off my scarf, my coat, my jacket, my tie, my watch, my cuff links, my shoes, and my socks, inspected the mail, poured a drink, and was running a bath when the interphone rang. It was Julio. The cleaner.

Of course I helped him. Not that I really wanted to, but I could not decently watch the poor guy carting off all my family's dirty laundry without giving him a hand. And besides, as my wife would confirm: I'm a monster, but I'm kind, all the same. Kind.

Because Julio and I were monopolizing the elevator, you eventually decided to use the stairs and walk up six flights, at your own pace.

*

You were out of breath when you finally arrived. You were not young anymore and you had a lot to carry: two thick files under your left arm, and a wicker basket filled with food in your right hand. A basket bursting with branches of celery and leek. I recall this because it was so unexpected. I would never have imagined you doing anything remotely domestic. I don't know why. I simply couldn't imagine a man who wore derby buckle shoes making dinner. It's idiotic, but the leeks completely threw me, I have to admit.

(In my defense, let it be said that I was down to basics in those days. The strict minimum.)

So there we were, face-to-face in the middle of my dejection. I was barefoot, you were wearing Aubercy, and we greeted one another in our usual distracted manner. You didn't look at the elevator or my apartment even once, you just wove your way between two boxes and closed the door to your apartment behind you.

The efficient Julio had soon cleared the place out and the worst of it was that I couldn't stop myself from giving him a tip. I didn't even think about it, it's second nature with me. I always say thank you, and I always thank people with money. I can hear the sentiment sycophants tut-tutting in protest all the way from here. I've been hearing them my entire life. The thing was, with Julio, it seemed to me that a fifty euro note slipped inside a little thank you would please him as much as a big verbal *thank you* slipped inside nothing at all. And his morality has nothing to do with it.

Nor does mine, for that matter.

All my life, I've been made to feel guilty for making money. And for using it as a shortcut with things and with people. For wanting to buy everything, above all proof of affection. I have never known how to cope. Honestly, I don't know what to say. I know how to make money the way others know how to spend it, and I give it easily because I know how useful it can be, it's as simple as that. Because of the price of our shoes, we've often touched on the subject (we never got into anything, but we touched on almost everything) and you always maintained that those right-thinking people were far more obsessed with cash than I was. "You are above all suspicion, my dear Paul. For you, money has no value," you insisted, "since you were born with it. Those people are obtuse. Forget it. Forget those flunkeys. Drop it," and when it was no longer enough to console me for being so misunderstood, you would always end up banishing the clouds by quoting Alphonse Allais:

"No need to take ourselves seriously; there will be no survivors."

(Forgive me, my dear Louis, but I am making the most of this last night with you to pour out my feelings a bit more than usual.) (It must be the altitude.)

Julio cleaned the place out, as I said, and I closed the door behind him the way you had closed your own door a few minutes earlier.

This next bit is hard to tell. To give a fair rendering of things, I would have to use words I don't know how to handle. I was never taught them. Or never wanted to learn them. Cowardly words, too corruptible and unreliable. Too easily handled, to be precise. And it was because I was this . . . inmate, this emotionally incarcerated inner self, this total jerk, that I had reached this precise moment in my life.

I was fifty-four years old, I was running a company my great-grandfather founded. I was the only son. My father had killed himself at the controls of his plane when I was ten years old; my mother, the regent, had finally abdicated and was wallowing in Alzheimer's disease with delight, my first wife had taken our eldest son and gone to the United States, the second one had just left me, with our two daughters, for a "considerate" man (and the distance seemed even more terrifying), and the water in my bath was getting cold. There. That's it.

That is all I had to say.

I don't know how long I'd been standing dazed by the . . . I don't know, I was in the dark when a knock came at the door.

I hastily threw on a more or less presentable mask in the shape of a face, but in my haste I must have put it on upside down because I saw you, the way your face fell for a split second before you got your wits about you, your impassive face, in other words, and you announced:

"Homemade soup. A 2009 Mission Haut-Brion. Humphrey Bogart and Audrey Hepburn."

I was utterly speechless.

"Dinner in ten minutes. I'll leave the door ajar. See you soon."

And you turned on your heels.

Oh, thank you, Louis. Thank you.

Thank you, because your tone was so calm and peremptory that I immediately felt like a little boy who's been told to go and wash his hands.

How simple everything suddenly became.

Dinner . . .

I was being summoned.

So I headed to the bathroom and started by splashing my face with cold water and I . . . I am reluctant to relate these things. It takes so much out of me. And I . . . And it melted. The mask melted. Something in my hands melted.

Someone . . . Anyway. Let's move on. Water, water, everywhere, dixit the famous English poet.

I took off my shirt, rubbed my arms, chest, neck, shoulders, and navel; I eventually stood up straight and I recognized him. I recognized the little Cailley heir who did not have the right to weep in public. Enough, Paul, enough. Remember, life has been very good to you.

Beneath his crust, his rind, completely raw, I recognized him, in that very mirror that had witnessed his wife skinning him alive a few hours earlier.

Yes. Thank you, Louis. Thank you for having allowed me this: to strip myself bare at last.

* * *

Your apartment was plunged in shadows. I walked down a corridor, guided by the light of the candles you had arranged on a low table amid the jumble of bookshelves, books, files, loose papers, and piles of old newspapers that must have been your living room.

In front of a deep sofa, a table was set for two. Neat tablecloth, two soup bowls set on two plates, two silver soup spoons, two wine glasses, a bottle waiting to reach room temperature, a piece of cheese on a little wooden chopping board, and a basket of bread.

I heard your voice in the distance telling me to sit down, and you came out wearing an apron and carrying a steaming tureen of soup.

With the help of a big, antique ladle, you gave me a hearty serving, ground a bit of pepper over my bowl, then filled my glass.

Then you untied your apron, settled into the sofa next to me, sighed with pleasure, raised your glass to your nose, sniffed it, smiled, picked up the remote control, and asked me if I needed subtitles. I shook my head, you pressed play, *Sabrina* began, and you said bon appétit.

And so we feasted with the ravishing Audrey who, how appropriately, had just returned from the best culinary school in Paris.
Delightful. Delightful.
Violins, romance, we finished off the Beaufort and the bottle. You walked me to the front door in silence then wished me good night and invited me to come again the next day, at the same time.

I was so groggy I hardly thanked you.
Against all expectation I slept well that night. Really, really well.
(As things stand, I may as well confess to this solitary pleasure: I fell asleep thinking about your lovely slippers.) (Shipton & Heneage, *Grecian slippers*, you confessed, a few weeks later.)

Thank you, Louis. Thank you.
Thank you.
I don't know yet how many times I'll go on repeating myself, I'll count them at the end. And there will be as many thank yous as ~~handfuls of earth~~ as it takes.

The next evening there was cream of pumpkin. And it was the next evening that I understood why I was there. After the same ritual as the previous day, you turned to me, remote control in hand, and asked, looking vaguely concerned:
"I thought we'd watch *The Apartment*, but I don't want to seem tactless. Perhaps it's a bit too soon, what do you think?"
What a beautiful smile.
"No, it's perfect," I answered, full of wonder. "Perfect."

Louis. No one had ever taken care of me in this way. No one. Did I remember to say thank you?

(Once, just once in my life I was nurtured in this way, with the same absolute toughness and tenderness, just once. It was Emilia, little Emmie, the Alsatian maid who worked for my grandmother at La Huchaude, a sinister house in the Nivernais where just after my father died I spent an entire summer left to my own devices. When I was alone in the "château," as she put it, she let me have supper with her in the pantry and she made me French toast, dipping slices of a thick, four-pound, well-hardened bread into some curious batter of milk, sugar, and cinnamon.

(I will never forget the taste of that French toast. Never. It was the taste of kindness, simplicity, and disinterest. The type of dish I have not often eaten since.

(Yaya . . . Yaya would not let me speak when it was time for her serial on the radio. Yaya to whom I practiced reading, over and over, the passage in Jules Verne's novel where Michel Strogoff is sentenced "never to see the things of the earth," as he is about to be blinded by a white-hot saber. I practiced rolling my "r"s like the evil Ogareff so that his voice would sound crrrueller and even morrre terrrible. She loved it. A few months later I found out, completely by chance, that she had been dismissed, and when at last I dared ask my grandmother why (and to do so I had to show the same courage as the proud courier for the tsar), she simply answered that she, Yaya, "didn't always smell very nice.")

(Louis? Is this too much? Am I imposing on your eternity with my childish whining? If so, you only have yourself to blame, my friend, I didn't even remember that I remembered Yaya, and were it not for you I probably never would have remembered.)

This ritual—soup, fine wines, and Hollywood classics—lasted until the early hours of the following year. Every evening you set our appointment for the next one, and every evening that followed, I would come back to our confirmed old bachelors' tea party with an inexpressible sense of relief. (Inexpressible, adj. *That which cannot be said with or translated into words due to its intense, strange, or extraordinary nature.*)

Neither one of us made the slightest reference to Christmas or New Year's.

Since you were so kind as to renew your invitation from one evening to the next and I was in no fit state to decline it, we went on living as if nothing had happened. Or rather, as if nothing had happened and I went on living. My son went skiing in Colorado with his mother and dashing stepfather as planned, while Ariane and the girls frolicked in their swimsuits by a coral reef (I didn't try to find out whether the considerate man had gone with them, my apparent indifference would serve, I had decided, as an amiable gift I was giving myself) and you, without realizing it, became my only family and my only refuge.

What you thought about it, I don't know. I was careful not to ask you if you had nothing more entertaining to sink your teeth into, during this holiday period, than the resident cuckold. No, I didn't dare. And now, after all that's happened, I no longer know whether to be sorry for my lack of tact or, on the contrary, to be proud of it. Of course I did not wish to be seen to the door, but that wasn't all, Louis, that wasn't all. I respected your silence.

And even tonight, you know, if I am allowing myself to speak so shamelessly, it is solely because I am writing to you from the ends of the earth and in a state that is closer to sleepwalking than mere insomnia.

On Christmas Eve you'd put Frank Capra's *It's a Wonderful Life* on the program.

"Not a very original choice, and I'm sure you've already seen it a dozen times, but you'll see, it never gets old. And then this good little Clos-Vougeot will take care of the rest . . . "

I did not dare contradict you (I had never seen it) and I was very grateful to you for leaving us in the dark for a few seconds after the angel's final words. George Bailey's fate was like a fist in the gut, and I was not feeling very valiant when the time came to go home. So far from valiant, in fact, that I came and rang at your door a few minutes later.

"Did you forget something?"

"No, but I . . . You know I, I too, took over my father's business after he died and . . . "

And as I didn't know what else to say—well, I did, I knew very well but I did not know how to go about it—you put an end to my prevarication, waving it away with a burst of laughter.

"But of course I know, for goodness' sake! Everyone knows! You are at the helm of a flagship French industry! Off you go . . . Time for bed. All this emotion has worn us out."

At home again, sitting in the kitchen in my big, empty apartment, after the second glass of a superb whisky which one of my collaborators had given me that very morning, I was finally able to finish my sentence.

No one heard it, but what I was telling you went roughly:

" . . . I too took over my father's business after he died, and I too am acquainted with that solitude. That solitude, and the terrible fear of losing face. My enemy is not the despicable Potter, my enemy is the end of a world, of my world, the world I represent. My enemy is globalization, it's Asia, where at this very moment I have wandered astray, it's delocalization. My enemy has already beaten me. 'Flagship French industry.' My

dear Louis . . . there has been no such thing as French industry for a long time. I am no longer expanding my company, I
am simply avoiding its loss. I am saving the family jewels. Or
selling them off cheap, rather. The feet of the colossus are
made of clay, and . . . "

And a few sips later,

" . . . and I'm alone. Far more alone than George Bailey ever
was, because I've never done anything good for those around
me, I . . . I've never known, even fortuitously, how to make
myself loved the way he did, because I've never known how to
love, either. As cynical as it might seem, I've never had the
means. I've often been told that I was born with a caul, but
what sort of caul, for God's sake? A spiked helmet? A leaden
miter? I wasn't born with a caul, I was born crippled. And at
this time of reckoning, not only is my wife hardly raising the
alarm to save me from drowning, she has gone off who knows
where to toast her buns, keeping my kids from me on
Christmas day. As for friends, what of them? What friends?
What are we talking about? I don't even know how a friend is
made. Are they designed? Modeled? Tested? Copied at lower
cost? Patented?"

Okay. I was drunk.

And because I was drunk, I was finally able to finish my
sentence:

" . . . no, I didn't have time for anything. And I'm alone on
earth. But this evening you are still here, my stranger of a
neighbor who does not speak, who asks for nothing, who I
always approach empty-handed, something that had never
happened to me in my entire life, who I always approach
empty-handed because I too am so empty, so empty, so dis-
heartened and powerless that I don't even have a nickel's
worth of politeness to offer, and . . . "

And shit. Another sip:

" . . . and . . . and it's not my community that grabbed me

by the collar one evening of despair by the parapet, it was you. It was you who saved me."

I'm crying, Louis. I'm crying over myself.

Too much! Listen to this scoundrel, muddling your funeral oration! It's a good thing that ridicule doesn't kill us, either . . .

Your soup has made me hungry.
Don't go, let me put you on hold, just long enough to get room service.

* * *

Almost three o'clock, I gobbled down my bowl of bibimbap (rice, stir-fried vegetables, fried egg, red pepper paste) standing at the window.

Over ten million inhabitants and no one seems to be asleep. Offices, buildings, advertising screens, Seoul Tower, traffic, avenues, garbage trucks, bridges, it's all twinkling. No, sorry, shining. No moon, not even a single star. From this high up and for as far as I can see, there is nothing that is not artificial. Everything shines. Everything blinks.

(I've noticed that the hotel rooms in these monster cities, whatever the continent, always act as an inner seismograph for me. When I'm feeling good, I admire the ingenuity of mankind and could spend hours studying its accomplishments; and when I'm not as valiant, like this evening, it all seizes me by the throat and I look away, staggering.

(What have we done? Where are we headed? How will it all end?)

Okay, hey there Mister holy moly preacher man, bring back Louis or go to bed.

Billy Wilder, Ernst Lubitsch, Frank Capra, Stanley Donen, Vincente Minnelli: we made it through the Christmas break like kids in the finest candy store in the history of cinema and bit by bit, every evening, by dint of encountering the same old regulars in the same little neighborhood movie theater, we struck up a conversation.

Initially we started out in movie-lover mode. We'd comment on the directing, the screenplay, the producers, the on-set anecdotes, the actors and actresses (you were crazy about Audrey's neck, everyone else was merely entertaining), and from one film to the next, one reel leading to another, we got around to us. Well, us . . . the guy version of us. Meaning words that didn't have much to do with our selves. Subjects as diverse and varied as: our work, our career, our job, our work, our profession, our sector, our part, in short, our corporate name.

Corporate name which, in the light of the exciting little end-of-year soirées we were currently enjoying, could equally, easily also signify our reason for living, but oh well . . . we were too busy tossing confetti in each other's faces and strutting along like idiots doing the Chicken Dance to dare to point this out to each other.

(The truth is that you and I were entrenched in our positions, observing the front line through the chinks left by Audrey, Shirley, Ginger, Marlene, Lauren, Jane, Cyd, Leslie, Debbie, Rita, Greta, Gloria, Barbara, Katharine, and Marilyn.

(You have to admit that as sandbags go, you've seen worse . . .)

We had each begun to turn to our neighbor in the next seat when the lights came back on, and as the evenings went by, and the wine got better and better, and the cracks in our armor began to show, and our tongues loosened, we screened our own, personal films.

Our Seven Year Itches, Roads to Glory, O. Henry's Full Houses, Haves and Have Nots, Sunset Boulevards, Double Indemnities, Big Sleeps, and Aces in the Hole.

The more we kept our private lives at a distance, the more we revealed of ourselves—because our reasons for living, as hopeless as they might seem, said a lot about us in the end. Said everything.

Your gown, your specialization, your files, your cases; my toga, my background, my files, my worries; what more could we add to all that?

Nothing.

Our life. Those were our lives.

Hey, Cailley-Pompom, have you listened to yourself? All your pseudo-Hollywood metaphors, your lah-de-dah flights of fancy, your dashes and ellipses and semicolons and pretentious rhetoric? Can't you talk a little plainer, dude?

Well, uh . . . okay, then . . . well, actually, Louie and me were starting to get real wasted so we started to come unbuttoned. And the more we waved our dicks around, the more we could see it was nothing to shout about and that it wasn't even worth telling, specially as we were right in the middle of the holiday cheer and there we were two old farts eating our tapioca and watching movies we already knew by heart and . . .

Hey . . .

You see my index finger? You see how good it is at pointing the way to Santa Claus's house?

I don't know about you, Louis, I can't speak for you, but for me, I'll tell you straight out: this was the best break in my entire life.

And even. Even. If I dared. If I was really absolutely sure

you were dead forever. Maybe then. Maybe I would say it: it was the break of a lifetime, my lifetime.

Christmas is never much fun when you're an only child, and when on top of it you become an orphan, it really begins to smell a bit off—whiffs of slavery, imprisonment, that sort of thing—so if to boot you get saddled first with a traumatlantic divorce, then a separation as tough as a Christmas capon stuffed with dry, stale bread, and kids who allegedly have been contaminated by your stress, and a considerate lover . . . How should I put it? All that merry piping of the shepherd in the crèche, and the New Year's resolutions, well, it all seemed better at your place.

More honest.

I have been a bad son, a bad husband, and a bad father, I know. It's a fact. It's factual. But . . . No. No buts. I'm not writing to you tonight to justify myself. So, no buts. But still. And. Therefore. It just so happens that.

It just so happens that I was brought up without love. I was brought up without love and you cannot imagine what it's like growing up all alone, never having your fill of . . . I don't know . . . your fill of embraces: you're forever left with something hard and awkward.

I have been, and still am, a hard, awkward man.

And, therefore, it just so happens that I was educated, no, sorry, trained to ensure the continuity of a company that I did not found, but which ensured the room and board (and perhaps even, who knows? the care, education, peace—a certain peace, let's say, the relative material peace) of thousands of people.

That, too, is fact. Bad husband, bad son, and bad father, but in the meantime, no one is going hungry. Everyone eats their fill. Everyone.

If I had boarded the plane as planned; if I'd had a better grade on my history paper, if I'd known who Pepin the Short was, what he founded, and who his son was, if my father had not punished me by not allowing me to go with him on the flight as planned, I would have died, too. I would be buried next to him in a ridiculous mausoleum, and those thousands of people I mentioned just now might not have been any worse off, but in the meantime, I'm the one who stepped up to the plate. Me. And no one asked me my opinion.

And everyone has food on their plate.

The rest I could not deal with. I didn't know how to lead a professional life and a private life at the same time. I knew I was better equipped, and only equipped, for the former, and more or less consciously—depending on whether life seemed to distract me from it or not—I tended to favor my professional life.

These are details I am not proud of, and I alone am aware of them, but I know this for a fact: I know I favored my professional life because it seemed easier, more convenient, no, not more convenient, that's not the house style—more feasible.

I favored hardness and awkwardness to transform these handicaps into assets. I favored whatever put me at less of a disadvantage. And . . . And so that was where I had ended up, that was what I brooded over, those nights after I left you and found myself freewheeling through despondency.

I realized that in your home, even though you lived alone, there was life, and life felt loved. At my place, there was no more life.

I still don't know why you held out your hand to me, Louis; you never told me, but what I do know is that our winter respite did me a lot of good. "Eat your soup so you can grow up to be big and strong," is what real mothers say and . . . Thank you for the soup, neighbor. Thank you for the soup, hearty or velouté—not to mention all your wizard's gruel. I was already too old to grow up to be big and strong, alas, but you helped me stand up straight, straighten my spine, re-vertebrate me and make me taller by . . . what . . . a good little half-inch, maybe.

A little half-inch and the desire, the need, rather, the necessity of prolonging the cease-fire within myself.

Pepin the Short was king of the Franks, he founded the dynasty of the Carolingians and he was the father of Charlemagne. Right, and now that I've remembered, I can forget it again, can't I?

Frankly, what the hell do I care about Pepin the Short?

Our New Year's Eve was perfect.

The night before, I didn't visit, and I was late that evening because I'd had to do the rounds to thank all the employees at headquarters and the French facilities for the year gone by. (I don't like holiday wishes. Too pious; too worldly.) Tsk, tsk, bad father, but good paternalistic boss; I can hear the tongues wagging already. Yes. It's true. Good, paternalistic boss. Visit the offices, distract them on each floor, tour the workshops, break the pace, go up into the watchtowers, look at faces, shake hands, look into their eyes, understand things, take note of them in a corner of my brain, don't forget them, don't forget anyone, go down to the parking lot and greet them there too, these people you never see, don't make a big deal of it, don't even make a deal at all. Just, here I am. I'm just passing by. I came by. I'm your good old long-suffering jerk of a boss, for sure, but in the meanwhile, see for yourselves: I came by. I remember that you do exist, that's all. That is all I had to say to you: I remember.

I was late, I realized, and I hadn't even bothered to change my shirt, whereas you had gotten out your best apron and you stood before the raft that served as our sofa, with a big tray in your hands.

On the tray there were two white bowls, each one topped with a dome of flaky pastry.

You set the tray down, cleared your throat, and announced, gravely, one hand folded behind your back:

"Tonight we have *soupe à la truffe*. A dish created in 1975 by Monsieur Paul Bocuse the day he was awarded his Légion d'Honneur, for a luncheon given at the Elysée Palace by Monsieur Valéry Giscard d'Estaing, President of the Republic at that time, and his wife, the vivacious Anne-Aymone."

And there, I had to laugh. I laughed because your apron was imprinted with the trompe-l'oeil bosom of a sublimely vulgar and virtually naked creature (a few tassels at the most, a few tassels, a few bits of turquoise and a few eagle's feathers) sitting with her thighs spread wide behind the handlebars of a Harley.

I laughed and you smiled.

That was our mistletoe.

You were in great spirits that evening, you had *Singin' in the Rain* on the program, I think you'd had a little to drink while waiting for me and once the film was over, you murmured:

"I have a confession to make . . . "

I hated the tone of your voice. I had no desire to hear some confession. I hated confessions. They terrified me. We had gotten along fine up to that point without lapsing into sentimentalism, so why go and spoil everything?

"I'm listening," I said, stiffening.

"Well, can you imagine that this old fart here . . . Yes, yours truly . . . This rusty old beanpole hunched over here before you was elected best tap dancer at Harvard's Fred & Ginger's Club in the summer of nineteen hundred and . . . well, of his generation, in other words."

"Really?" I said, relaxing.

"Don't move."

You stood up straight.

"I'd like you to know, Paul," (he was a bit drunk), "to . . . to know that . . . that you weren't the only person in favor of exporting all things French. No, no, no! I too took part in the scheme to promote our country, old man! I too hoisted the flag! Don't move: let me show you how high a French froggy can jump!"

He came back wearing a pair of old red, white, and blue shoes.

"And now," (drum roll of little spoons on his grandfather's bronze skull), "ladies and gentlemen . . . Oh, no, damn—and now, gentleman only, for your astounded eyes only, the world-famous Froggy Loo-isss presenting his even more world-famous tap-dancing number!"

And then . . .

The dancing lunatic.

Fred Astaire and Gene Kelly, all to myself. Slightly rusty, slightly tipsy, to be sure, but all to myself. The rattle of little metallic taps on Baron Haussmann's parquet floor.

The clatter, click, song, melody, even, yes, melody of little taps on the old baron's parquet floor, while we could hear the far-off muffled crackling of some fireworks set off who knows where.

From a distance (but I really was sitting way at the back of the sofa), there was a touch of *An American in Paris* about it all.

Then you showed me the technique for tapping to one

beatcount, two beatcounts, three, then . . . Well no, you weren't able to do the other combinations, you collapsed again next to your dazed and astounded audience.

Ah, Louis. It did come to a hell of a good end, that annus horribilis. One hell of a good end.

All the more of an ending in that when we parted, a few moments later, we made it clear to each other, without having to say a word, that now, gentleman and gentleman, lights out, the show was over.

Reels rewound and umbrellas snapped shut.

For the first time I shook your hand and, for the first time, you walked me back to my front door.

I said, a bit solemnly, I think: "Thank you, Louis. Thank you."

You waved it away with the back of your hand, my surfeit of solemnity, and said, looking me straight in the eyes:

"You'll be fine. You'll see: it will all be fine."

I nodded, just the way little Paul with his dirty hands would have done that first evening, and you went away with a charming tap tap tick-a-tock—a little Hollywood entrechat, of the made-in-France variety.

* * *

The next day, January first, I went to see my mother in her chic medical hospice.

Of course she didn't recognize me. Any more than on any of the previous visits.

She gazed fixedly at the stranger sitting at the end of her bed and we had an Into-the-Void Staring Contest for a long while, until I eventually broke the silence.

"You know, I've made a friend."

She didn't react.

She didn't react and it didn't matter at all, it still did me good. At least for once in my life I will have managed to have some sort of complicity with her.

So I went on.

"His name is Louis, he's very kind, and he tap dances."

To hear myself saying such silly, simple, childish words, on a public holiday, to a woman who had at last become human— but only once her brain had turned to porridge, reflecting a more or less legible image of a mother to me at last: it made me want to laugh and cry at the same time.

By then I didn't know anymore.

I didn't know. I was lost.

By then I was so clueless about everything that I stayed with her much longer than usual. It was quiet, I felt good, I was steeped in calm. I looked at her. I looked at her face, her neck, her long, useless arms, her hands, and I thought, Take a good look at her because you won't be coming back. You won't set foot in this room again. And she doesn't know you, she doesn't recognize you anymore, and now it's like the business with the Carolingians, now it's too late, there's no point trying to remember anymore.

Look at her one last time and then do like Louis showed you. Shuffle, brush, step, and tap, transferring all your weight onto the tap. Make it ring out, Paul, make it ring out. Look at her one last time then leave this weightlessness behind you.

* * *

The hostilities started up again but it was no longer the same. Even if we saw very little of each other in the weeks and months that followed, I knew you were there, that goodness was there. It may seem a measly candle wick in a life as barren as mine, but I know what I mean. It was like in the awful antechamber where my mother was patiently waiting: the good was done, the good had been done. Suddenly all the rest did not weigh so heavily beneath the harness. The rest would follow. Everything had been changed. Audrey had been there.

As for Ariane, she never came back, but our relations were warmer. The pretext being, of course, the girls, the girls and their logistics, and it was a fine pretext. I'd been incapable of giving them a happy family life and I was still just as awkward, but they knew that already. They knew it and had learned to live with it. As a result, they took good care of their great lump of a dad. They took him every other weekend, the occasional Wednesday evening when he was around, and during vacation. They dressed him, went out with him, took him to the Jardin d'Acclimatation or the zoo at Vincennes. They showed him how to send balloons and fireworks and confetti via text message, they taught him how to decrypt the subtleties of emoticon language, how to watch makeup tutorials, play Harvest Moon DS, find Sprites, buy the teleportation stone, build a bird shed, save the harvest goddess, change his profile picture, unfriend fake friends, like funny Youtubers, stop going to the restaurant all the time, and slice coagulated overcooked macaroni noodles into equal portions.

Above all they showed him a path away from the path of guilt. Another path, a detour, a shortcut. An amnesty. Okay, he hadn't done the job properly and some of his failings could never be repaired, but for now he was the one who'd gotten the miracle glove at the Harvest Sprite Casino.

No, you and I didn't see much of each other anymore, until one evening, you got things going again. You saw us on the landing and you invited us to come to the cinema at your place.

O tempora, o mores, truffles had been replaced by sushi and Julia certainly was not dressed by Givenchy, but you loved *Pretty Woman* and the girls loved it with you.

A new cine-club was born: every other Saturday evening, if Louis was around, we would go to his place. You introduced them to Paul Grimault and they gave you Hayao Miyazaki in exchange. You gave them Buster Keaton, and they lent you Buzz Lightyear. You gave them all of Jacques Demy and they arrived with the entire Studio Ghibli in return. They loved coming to your place. They loved your mess, your canes, your Daumier prints, your paper cutters and your glass paper-weights. They said, "Why do you keep all those old newspapers all over the floor?" and you lowered your voice and said, "Because there are little mice that live underneath, you see . . . " and then it was ever so hard to concentrate on the movie . . . So, so hard . . . With one eye they wept for *E.T.* and with the other they were watching out for the least little rippling under the surface of those old forgotten issues of *Le Monde.*

But it all remained very tenuous, very sober. Both of us were unsociable, we had both received the same good upbring-ing, give or take, that teaches paralysis as surely as it does politeness, and we were always afraid we might be disturbing one another.

Particularly me. I kept my distance. You were a man of dossiers, I knew you worked at home a lot, and I was very scrupulous about such things. (Work! The God Work!) And then there were your absences. Your nights of carousing, you called them. Your nights of great murkiness. You led a com-plicated life, Louis, didn't you? Well, complicated, perhaps not, but full of contrasts, let's say, full of contrasts.

Because of all this—your dossiers, your solitude, your ellipses—I might have left things there, with the truce we'd established back then, and would already have considered myself lucky, but our shoes, once again, trampled all our good manners underfoot.

I can't remember when, or how, or whose idea it was, but it became, in addition to our mouse and sushi sessions with the girls, our new confirmed old bachelors' ritual. On Sunday evenings, when I was alone and you were "fasting" (that was the word you used) we would polish our shoes together.

Like those car trips that give you the illusion that the only thing that lies ahead is the road, or those steep hikes that require you to keep a close watch on your feet through the difficult stretches, or like snapping the ends off green beans when, between two abrupt little gestures, you have to look out for the string—like any manual activity you are performing together with someone at the same time, in fact, polishing shoes is a wonderful way to get to know the other person, without letting anything on.

We removed the laces, cleaned, applied the polish, spread it, impregnated the leather, nourished, polished, rubbed, brushed, shined, sheened, and put the laces back in and, incidentally, fortuitously, during these various operations which provided us with a cover, since they monopolized all our attention, incidentally, as I was saying, we chewed the fat.

In the beginning we would always talk about the merchandise (our shoes, past, present, and future), then we talked shop (our work weeks, past, present, and future), and finally, we discussed productivity (God, Life, Solitude, Death; past, present, and future).

We spoke about our leathers at least as much as we took care of them, and our final strokes of polish often took us far away from our hidebound reality.

Shoe upon shoe, pair after pair, we learned to understand the other person's mechanisms and his modus operandi, but as we were also very discreet, we neglected to . . . no, not neglected, not eluded, either, we respected, observed, rather, yes, that's the word, *observed*, the way one observes a rule, a rite, a minute of silence, or a fast, precisely, we also, alas, observed their commandments and we never got our hands dirty.

We were familiar with each other's mechanisms, but we knew nothing about the combustion, fuel, or wear and tear, and I regret that bitterly, now.

I regret it bitterly because the news of your death came as a terrible shock.

I didn't know you were sick, Louis. I didn't know that you'd been fighting your illness for years. There I was, living next door, I owed you so much, I would have done anything for you and I did not know a thing.

You were my friend of solitude, my late-come friend, my evening friend, my camp friend, my bivouac friend, maybe an imaginary friend, but my friend all the same. The friend I did not have time to get to know.

(I wrote *love* and then thought better of it, yet again.) (What a jerk.)

The friend I didn't have time to love and appreciate. (What a jerk, as I said.)

Of course two years is not a long time and we didn't see each other that often. All told, not counting the films, the girls, the movement of the brushes, and the merely polite pleasantries, our hours in each other's presence did not add up to that many, in the end, and . . .

And the news of your death was a terrible blow.

You often vanished. Sometimes for a long time. You were out in the country, or so you told the girls. You went to take your mice for a walk. And then one day you didn't come back.

One day you didn't come back, at all, and another day, Lucie, my youngest daughter, through Laure, her sister, through Ariane, their mother, through Mako, their nanny, and through Fernanda, our concierge, told me that there was no point waiting for you to watch *Grave of the Fireflies,* that you, too, were in heaven, that you would never come back again, that . . . but what would become of the little mice?

I learned of your death through a rosary of ladies.

I was your friend and I heard about your death from the concierge.

There's a slap in your face, Paul, poor little rich boy.

A slap for the dominant male, distributor of Christmas envelopes, lord of the gratuities.

A whopping great slap, right in the face.

You see, you went on perfecting my education right to the end.

Then came the rumors that you had committed . . . that you had ended your own life. I wasn't interested. I paid no attention to those rumors. I am grateful to you for this and respect you all the more for it. Suicide, too, is my imaginary friend. I merely lost my half-inch again, from bending to the weight of my remorse.

The thought that perhaps you reached the end of your suffering by inflicting yet greater suffering on yourself: it made me wretched. I could have, should have, helped you, would have liked to. In any way I could. In every way.

I could have obtained the details regarding your passing, but I didn't want to know. You wanted to leave so you left, that was all that mattered. To me. That consoled me.

* * *

Louis,

One day you left for the country with your mice, another day a little girl in tears told me you were dead, and yet another day, much later, people came to empty your apartment, and that very evening a big boy smelling of sweat rang at my door and handed me a cardboard box. I recognized your handwriting on it: *for the neighbor across the landing* and, in the box, there was a wooden wine crate.

A Château-Haut-Brion crate, in memory of your first mission.

Since we'd drunk them together, there were no more bottles in the crate, but there were 2 horsehair brushes (one for light polish, the other for dark), 2 boar bristle brushes for shining, 2 little toothbrushy things in boar bristle for the welts and the sneakier spots, 4 jars of polish, 4 boxes of shoe wax to go with the polish, a nourishing milk, a suede brush, a suede block, some terre de Sommières stain remover, and a soft rag cut from an old shirt that I recognized. I'd seen you wear it. Maybe it hadn't been even that old. But it was soft, that much was certain. It was soft and it acted as the farewell note that you hadn't been able, or willing, to write.

It was so soft I blew my nose in it.

I took your departure very badly, Louis, secretly and badly. There, too, I don't know which had it worse, my pride, or my flesh (my heart, moron, my heart), but for a long time I remained in the state I described to you at the beginning of this letter. What was it I said? A wedge. That's right, a wedge. A wedge someone had rammed into my skull, all the way at the top, in the middle, where the fontanelle closes over.

I've always suffered from terrible migraines—and you knew

this, because one evening you saw me completely out of it; you saw me lie down on your floor with my head in my hands, you saw me collapse on your bed of newspapers like a huge bundle of pain, you heard me beg you to switch everything off, to be quiet, to make everything quiet, shut everything up, turn off all the lights, make it completely dark, stop all motion, don't move a thing, dip a napkin in ice water and put it on my face like a compress. Later, once the crisis was over, you heard me explain to you that it was like an enucleation, an evil spirit with a tiny but deep spoon with nice sharp edges was there behind my eye sockets using all his weight as a lever to turn the handle of his instrument of torture, first one way then the other, ever so slowly and conscientiously, to dig the eye out of its socket; and that these crises were so sudden, implacable, and violent that I could have blown my brains out a dozen, a hundred times, already—yes, I've always had terrible migraines and now, as if that weren't enough, I've got your death rammed into my brainpan.

I'm going to take a shower. I'll be back.

scorching water
for a long, long, long time

melted
drained
dissolved
scraped
liquefied
liquidated

Liquidated, the old man. Liquidated.

That's better.

Daybreak. I have to hurry.

If I brought up these episodes of descent into hell just now, it wasn't to make you feel sorry for me, Louis, it was to get myself back on my feet.

I don't have time to go hunting for words anymore. I have to leave in less than two hours and I'm still in my bath towel.

I don't have time for anything anymore, just to get myself back on my feet before I toss some ash on the embers and strike camp.

My feet, you remember, that's—cut and paste—"a woman full of wit to whom I had just related our early-morning to-ings and fro-ings (I will tell you later the circumstances thereof), emphasizing the strange comfort they gave me."

Yes. The same. The woman who would call out to Proust in the street and ask him if he was on the way home from the Duchesse de Guermantes's place, or from a urinal.

It was because of her that we have spent this night together, you and I.

Because of or thanks to, I'm not sure which, but what is certain is that were it not for her—her irony and clear-sightedness and talent—were it not for Proust and his admirer Morand, I wouldn't have done it.

I wouldn't have gone rapping at the door of the dead. I would have gone no further than *Untitled 1*, and *"you piss me off,"* and I would never have said another word to you. Or as few as possible.

I'm not sure you would have gained much in exchange, but this time I won't sign off with a coarse remark.

You don't piss me off, Louis. You don't piss me off at all.

So, the circumstances.

Let's talk about the circumstances.

I was at an airport. Indeed. Fate. I was in a gigantic terminal at London Heathrow and I had a meltdown.

Noise, sounds, crowds, bright light everywhere, neon lights, voices calling, music, people, smells, engines, machines, metal detectors, beeps, colors, movement, waves, sirens, espresso machines, heating, air conditioning, the stink of airplane fuel, ringing, telephones, cries, laughter, children, I thought I would die from the pain.

I was standing behind a pillar, with my forehead on it, ready to step back and smash it open at last. Like an egg, a keg, a rotten pumpkin, a coconut: smash the thing, once and for all.

I was stifling, sweating, dripping, shivering, I peeled off layers of clothes, my teeth were chattering.

I came round in a hospital room.

I'll spare you the details, but it was a long assault course, which I navigated ingloriously, and at the end of it the insurance companies and the banks ordered me to *seek therapy*. To strip down. Let myself be strip-searched. Soul-searched. See what science would have to say. Audit myself, in a way.

And at each consultation, I found myself sitting opposite a woman.

That woman.

I had nothing to say to her.

I didn't say a thing for two whole sessions.

At the beginning of the third one—which, we had both agreed, would be the last one, given my patent unwillingness to cooperate—she said:

"You know, if you don't like the term shrink, or therapist, because it feels incriminating to you, all you have to do is view me the way those patients of mine who are most resistant to any form of dishonest compromise view me, those patients we refer to as mad, crazy, nutcases, weirdos, all those Napoleons and so on. You know what they call me?"

She was being such an imperial pain in the ass that I felt like saying Josephine, but didn't dare.

"They call me the *head*-doctor," she replied with a smile. "Remind me why you're here, already?" (Eyeglasses, distracted look at my file.) "Ah, yes, your left knee . . . "

Ha ha ha. Very funny. Madame psychoanalyzing a clown.

I didn't respond.

She gave a sigh, closed my file, took off her pretty eyeglasses, and looked straight at me as if firing daggers.

"Listen to me, Paul Cailley-Ponthieu, listen carefully. You are wasting my time. So we are going to stop this session right now. Don't worry, I will sign the papers and discharge forms you need to go back into battle. Yes, I will do that for you: I am sending you back to the front because it's what you want, but since my professional conscience is just as rigorous as your own, I want you to take this."

She put her glasses back on, typed on her keyboard, leaned over, picked up the prescription that emerged from the printer, and handed it to me.

"There. Fit for duty. You will find a pharmacy on your left on the way out. Check in with reception regarding payment. Goodbye."

She stood up while I read her prescription:
Silistab Genu Patella Knee Brace x 1

She was on her feet. Looking at me.
I was seated. I was looking at my knees.

I was beginning to have a headache.

I felt like crying.

I was thirsty.

I was hot.

I began talking to her simply so I wouldn't weep.

I would still rather open this floodgate than that one.

I would still rather die with my mouth open than shed even one tear in front of this stranger.

So I opened my mouth and said your name.

And then I . . . And then nothing.

She didn't say anything either. Out of respect, I think. She saw me hopping from one foot to the other at the end of the diving board and refrained from giving me a shove from behind. That was kind.

After two or three long minutes had gone by, she gave me a little nudge all the same:

"Do you suffer from tinnitus? Do you have hearing problems?"

For a moment I was nonplussed. Then realized: your name, in French, is a homonym for hearing. Louis, l'ouïe.

"No," I laughed, drowning in my tears. "No. Louis. My friend Louis."

It was gushing out.

"Don't move," she said.

She left the room, then came back holding out a roll of kitchen towels.

"I'm sorry, that's all I have."

"Thank you."

She sat down in the armchair next to me while I mopped my face.

Silence.

Then she spoke to me the way she had to speak to me. She didn't say, "Yes . . . Of course . . . So, Louis . . . Louis . . . Your friend, you were saying . . . How interesting . . . But still . . . But how . . . But blah blah blah and how did you feel."

No.

She looked me straight in the eyes and said, calmly:

"My next appointment is in forty-five minutes. What do we do?"

She spoke about procedure, schedule, efficacy. She put me back in familiar territory.

I don't know exactly what I said, but I must have spoken about that way you had of being both intense and volatile at the same time, being absolutely present and yet always slightly elsewhere, both generous and stingy. About everything you had done for me, and the brutal way you'd died on me. The words of farewell I'd been deprived of. Your lack of trust. In me, in yourself, in our friendship. The nasty impression I kept getting, constantly chewing it over, that I had completely passed you by. Missed you altogether. Betrayed you. Betrayed myself. That I was a complete and utter failure.

Am a complete and utter failure.

Also, that I was an only child. That I had probably projected the image of an ideal brother onto you. I had dreamt you, invented you, made you up. It was not you I was weeping over, but my lovely hologram. I was weeping over a lot of deaths, in fact. Your death, the death of our friendship, of my father, of the adoring uncle you'd become to my daughters, the death of my fatherhood, of my filiation, of my childhood, my youth, and my own life, which had finally been taken from me and . . . And then I talked about your secrets, your absences, your silences, and what that morning vision of you inspired in me, when you were returning, as far as I could tell, from a world of liberty/tine/tinage, whereas I was on my way to wall myself up in a car that was as long and black as a hearse and which would take me to start my shift in a free-market liberticide world which I defended as best I could, while in fact in the space of a few years that same world had been destroying the combined efforts of four generations of men and women of good will, which included some bosses.

"Yes," I said again, "that's the image that haunts me. That vision of him, at dawn . . . So handsome, yet ravaged by the night, by illness, by solitude, by . . . I don't know."

"It sounds like Paul Morand calling out to Proust . . . "

I didn't react. I would rather be taken for a pedant than for an idiot.

There was no fooling her. She looked me straight in the eye for a long time, long enough to make me understand that I was, alas—no doubt about it, the proof being this long pause—a pedant of the worst kind: an idiot of a pedant. Then, once this had been made perfectly clear, she moved her face closer to mine and in her lovely, deep voice she added:

"Proust . . . What sort of soirée do you go to at night to come home with eyes so weary and lucid? And what fright, forbidden to us, did you have, to come back so indulgent and so kind?"

Silence.
Her: There was a bit of that, no?
Me: (Silence.)
Her: You have nothing to say?
I said nothing.
She looked at me for a moment longer, stood up, motioned to me to do the same, and walked me to the door.

"Let the receptionist know if you want to schedule another appointment or not, but in the meantime, allow me to say one important thing."

I wasn't listening anymore.

"Are you listening?" she said.

"Sorry. Yes."

"People live, have lived, and die, that's the way it is, and you . . . Are you still listening?"

"Yes."

"People live, and the only thing we remember after they have died, the only thing that matters, that stays with us, is their kindness."

I said nothing.

"Don't you agree?"

I didn't know what to say.

"Rather than brooding over what that man didn't give you, talk about his kindness."

"Talk to who? To you?"

"To me, if you come back here, to him if you don't."

"But he's dead."

"He's dead?"

I didn't answer.

"No. Of course he isn't. If he were dead you would have buried him already."

"He knew how kind he was."

"He knew? Are you sure?"

Silence.

"I don't know how to write."

"I didn't tell you to write, I told you to talk about him. The way you did just now, but addressing him instead. As if he were sitting there across from you. No need to take it any further than that: just talk to him."

I didn't know what to say.

"Talk to him and say goodbye."

I was silent.

"I am not being as authoritarian as usual, but now I know you won't come back here and I don't want to send you back to the enemy—to yourself, in other words—without a laissez-passer in your pocket."

What did she mean?

"Tell him everything you have on your mind and then let him go."

"This all seems very esoteric to me," I said, defensively, not managing a smile, "are you really a doctor?"

"No, but—"with a frank smile—"don't tell anyone, will you? Let's just say I'm making an effort to adapt and you, dear case number 1714, you have no business in a psychiatric service, you just need to express yourself."

I didn't know what to say.

"You're trying too hard, Paul. You're only making things worse. Stop it. Keep things simple. Say it like it is. OK, I have to go. I've got work."

I never went back.

* * *

I've just been informed that the driver is waiting downstairs. I have to get dressed. I have to go.

Louis,
You see? I'm back on my feet.

They told me you were dead. They asked me to bury you. I myself said just now that I would toss ashes on the embers before striking camp and . . .

But I won't. I won't strike camp. I have no desire to bury you. None at all.

No kisses goodbye, no hugs; I don't dare. I just—

Enough. Time to go.

A BOY

1

I was so out of it, leaving Saint-Jean-de-Luz, I almost missed the damn thing, took forever to reach my compartment, and when at last, after slowly and painfully making my way along the steep corridor, I managed to find my seat (when we reached Biarritz, roughly), I realized I was going to have to spend over five hours stuck in this fucking little cage and I wasn't even facing the engine.

Never mind.

I clung to my headrest for a long while.

I clung to it just to hang on, to keep from vomiting, to crouch down and think and chew over the pros and cons of such a disgrace.

(Round peg in a square hole, fuck.) (A square family.) (Window seat on top of it.) (Miles away from the bar.) (Straitjacket, in other words.) (The sobering up cell.) (The clink.)

Oh Jesus Mary and Joseph. Oh pigheaded idiot.

Where was I? Oh, yes, I was crouched over the carpet, ruminating, when someone tried to walk on my head with a suitcase with wheels.

Ouch.

There I was, drunk, wasted, hurting all over, I moaned and went to slump two seats further over.

This fucking grandma kicked me out in no time.

So I crawled over to the one opposite, and at the next station

(Bayonne) (or maybe it was Dax), an unidentified voice asked me, vaguely confused, if I wasn't in the wrong seat. By any chance.

What a calamity. I hadn't slept in three days, I'd been living it up, surfing, swimming, bachelor party with a buddy, then married him off to one of my exes, I'd been singing, dancing, laughing, drinking, smoking, jeering, I took stuff, turned on, got high, perched up there and pedaled through the Milky Way, rolled a spliff with Espelette pepper, lost my teeth, came back down, sinned, slept on the wharf, drank one last glass with my cousin at the station buffet, validated her pussy as I was getting up from my chair, apologized, jumped in the first railroad car I found, I was disorientated, stewed, brewing, fermenting, something was brewing, I was coming down with myxomatosis, I counted my teeth again and tried desperately to remember where I'd left my canine, my hair, my belt, the keys to my scooter, my watch, and my dignity. I had a conference call with my evil twin so he'd fix things for me, reception was poor and I really did not feel AT ALL like being roused from my alcoholic coma for a third time. So I went back to my basket, I mean my seat, without asking for my due.

I pissed off the three other passengers, treading on their feet and half collapsing in their laps as I made my way to my own wee little seat.

I snuggled against the armrest and put my forehead against the nice soft and sticky window.

Mmmm.

How good that felt.

Go to yer basky-wasket and curl up your pitty-paws, as my grandma used to say.

Because I'd just got woken up by this strange creature who

got on in Bayonne (or Dax), I closed my eyes, but I didn't get back to sleep right away.

I was drowsing. Daydreaming. I tried to zone out, on the sly, on the up and up, not counting too heavily on the sheep. I felt good, purring, my head wobbling, lulled by the clackety-clack of the rails.

For three days I'd been blasted and blitzed and now I was on the mine train roller coaster. I was puffing out my firedamp and chug-chugging along nice and quiet.

And in the distance, on another planet, out of sync and through a kind of grimy headset I could hear the real sounds of the real life of real people.

I'd been a DJ in my salad days and I was mixing my lullaby. I sampled all the sounds in car number 12 and distilled a real Zen sort of elevator Muzak using paracetamol and digestive tablets.

Tee-jee-vee's lounge.

2

I was settled in my seat, hugging myself, and rewinding the best moments of the weekend.

For three days I'd given my all because I was too old for all that stuff and I often got the sneaking suspicion that I was attending my own bachelor party, for the end of my youth . . . (too chubby for my old wetsuit) (too heavy for my old surfboard) (too rusty for those huge waves) (too stiff for those little wipeouts) (too young to die) (too old to be of interest to the hotties in the Bikini Contest) (too exhausted to hold my alcohol) (too full of alcohol to keep my distances) (too fat to play the Chippendale) (too lightweight for the father of the bride to have any regrets) (too slow for Basque *pelota*) (too wretched to pellet anyone at all) (too tired to get my rocks off) (too much of a sad sack to laugh about it) (too nothing) (too everything) (too nothing about everything), yes, I often had the suspicion that the jackoff's last hour had come. I was old.

Old, gray, sad, polluted.

Paris had gotten the better of me.

I was thirty-three, the same age as that guy with a bigger beard and more hair than me and who had given it all he'd got, far more than I ever would, and it was time, Lord Jesus, for me to take my destiny in hand and perform a few miracles, otherwise, at this rate, what I was attending wouldn't be a bachelor party but my own wake.

As I was saying, I was daydreaming and I smiled as I replayed those trailers in my mind.

. . . The way down in Nathan's car . . . The two guys we got matched with on BlaBlaCar to pay for our gas. One called Patrice (Patoche) we picked up at the Porte d'Orléans and the other, Momo (Mohammed) in Poitiers.

So, we gave Patoche a "Perfect" for his soundtrack (good music on his phone), (Motown, full blast), "Very good" for conversation (he kept his mouth shut), "Good" for conviviality (he paid for our coffees), "Disappointing" for driving (he'd used up all his points), and "To be avoided" for his look (short pants that ended halfway up his calf with an integrated zipper so they could be transformed into shorts in hot weather); and as for Momo, we rated him "Perfect" for everything (he slept like a log from pickup to drop-off) but "Disappointing" as a backing vocalist (The Supremes couldn't take his snoring).

Their heart can't take it no more.

. . . Arthur's bachelor party . . . Dinner for suave young men at the Grand Hôtel in Biarritz. We were all decked out like lords, then we took a ride along the corniche and the beer flowed freely at the Pandora club where a lissome young lady in a short dress undid our ties at the end then bound us all together again in her own way . . .

I was chuckling in the middle of my reverie.

. . . Then Camille arrived. My Camille, the Camille I had loved so, on her daddy's arm in the village church where we'd spent our first vacation, in love. The room her mom had prepared for us with very heavy sheets smelling of lavender, and roses on the night table. My lovely Camille. Camille, so pretty. My ravishing Camille, to the sound of the organ.

My Camille getting married in white but no longer a virgin, naughty girl. I knew this and her mom suspected as much, I think. She didn't say a word to her at breakfast.

. . . The pretty smile she sent me over the shoulder of her soon-to-be husband when she got close to the altar.
Tender. Radiant. Cruel.

The dance she honored me with at the end of the ball and the smiles I elicited from her only-just-turned husband, from the hairpins in her chignon . . . which was already coming apart, sort of. A bit loose.
Tender. Radiant. Cruel.

. . . Days on the beach. Sun, waves, friends. Some from the time we were kids. From the era of shrimping nets and the Little Shrimp Club.
Swimming, skylarking, blabbing, barbecues, our toasts to the local ham, to the Ossau-Iraty cheese, the rosé, love, the bride and groom, the cuckolds, and life.
Paddling out, more or less in line to attack the waves head-on, then returning like wet dogs. Vanquished, worn out, sheepish. Our tails in a twist and our wetsuits hanging limply between our legs.

. . . Our last fishing party, off our childhood jetty, and our last diving contest among the rocks, how it drove our mothers frantic.
. . . Our moms who were no longer there to box our ears after our exploits when we came home shivering with joy and terror. Our moms who used to drain the blue from our lips by rubbing our ears. Arthur's mom, who went back to the rented manor house because she was at loggerheads with the caterer (some sordid business about missing crates of

champagne) (uh-huh, uh-huh) and my own mother who didn't come to scold us that afternoon because a C-word (of the medical variety) had borne her away to other shores during the winter.

. . . My mom who'd been a schoolteacher, and if it hadn't been for her, said the groom again while slicing the cake, making us all weep, the ass, if it hadn't been for her he could never have written such a long and lovely speech.

. . . The last waffle with Arthur and his roommate before I left, where we stood licking our fingers very slowly and conscientiously while eyeing a school of young Spanish sardines out for a good time.

Our fingers covered with whipped cream and sea salt.

. . . Our . . .

Momo and the Supremes, my mistake, I think it was my own snoring that woke me up.

I could no longer hear myself dream.

My eyelids were all sticky, I ran my hand over my face to wipe off the cobwebs, and from the gob in my palm, I felt that I must have been drooling a fair amount between two borborygmi and three drunken burps.

Hey. Classy Joe.

I opened my eyes and immediately closed them again.

Dumbass.

There were two girls seated across from me. One ugly one who instantly looked down, chuckling to herself, and one hottie who glared at me before screwing in her earbuds with a sigh of exasperation.

Dumbass.

I didn't care about the ugly one, but the pretty one, that was too much.

I managed to catch a few more winks, just so I could piece together a more or less decent killer look and then I rejoined the game, my cards well in hand.

I sat up straight, tidied myself, tucked my shirt into my trousers, straightened my collar, combed my hair (gel made of zombie drool, guaranteed to hold), smoothed my eyebrows, ran my tongue over my lips that were dry from the booze and the salt spray, and set myself back in hunter-gatherer mode.

Hands back in my lap, a touch of disdain to mark a pause, eyes taking aim and smile running straight through.

I'm referring to the knockout, obviously. There was nothing to poach as far as the other girl was concerned, and besides, she had already been ambushed by her book.

The problem was that I was dying of thirst and desperate for a piss, but I didn't dare draw any more attention to myself with my secretions.

So I kept an eye on all that, wholeheartedly, but my heart wasn't in it. My heart was in my bladder.

Not focused, boy. Not at all focused. Or focused but bad: couldn't care less about the plain Jane, and the looker wasn't looking (at me).

Good, bad, okay. It happens.

Bad, but not only. There was something else bugging me.

My mom, as I said earlier when they were cutting the cake, had been a schoolteacher.

A super-Instructor, if you like, with a capital I, as in Illumination Intelligence, and Imagination, of which she had been the Inexhaustible Instigator her whole life long.

Books meant something in our house. A lot, even. And even today books mean a lot to me, in my life.

In the shabby hovel, where my old, immature, and tattered soul resides, most of the time, books and culture clean things out, prop them up, and even construct supporting walls, as they have done for as long as I can remember.

But here was something off balance: the pretty girl (superb skin, suntanned, eyes like agates, perfect nose, adorable mouth, hair begging to be caressed, breasts to die for, cheeks for kisses, lips for kisses, arms for kisses, body to, uh, be blessed) was reading crap (I'll let you imagine the worst) (no, no, even worse than that) (sort of pseudo-novel by a pseudo self-help guru for your genuine, suffering inner ninny) and the ugly girl (flat-chested, pale, emaciated, badly dressed, greenish hair, chewed-on lips, rough hands, nails in mourning, pierced eyebrow, pierced nose, wrists with tattoos, ears with studs, body worth defrocking) was reading the *Journal* of Eugène Delacroix.

Oh Cupid! Oh, naughty boy!
What a tease you are, with your little round buttocks!
What a tease, and how you play with the nerves of your poor, defenseless quarry . . .

The pretty girl was working on helping herself, checking the screen of her smartphone at every line break in her reading, while the ugly girl chewed on her right thumbnail (black), levitating in the pages of her book, oblivious of the outside world.

Because her lips were turning black, too, I figured it wasn't dirt she had under her nails but ink. India ink, probably. Yes, India ink. She had a huge spiral notebook on her lap as a tray, and a disgusting pouch was gaping open by the window. In the middle of so much disharmony, this made sense. This girl, at least, had found a suitable guru.

Right.

Time for that piss.

I disturbed all my fellow travelers and went to relieve myself.

As I emerged from my ablutions, hands and trousers equally damp (the place is so cramped and poorly maintained) wouldn't you know I went and slammed the door right into my explosive bombshell's hip.

Classy Joe is back.

I apologized, she ignored me and headed straight toward the lounge car.

I followed.

3

She may have been reading trash but she was really luscious, so I pulled out all the stops.

And all the stops with a nice boy like me who's been brought up by a feminine mom and a feminist dad, who knows how to recognize a Dior perfume, his faults, and an accent from Nice, and who was on his way home after three days by the seaside, believe me when I tell you it means pulling the pin on the explosive device in no time flat.

Well, no time, maybe not quite. Let's be honest. I had to pay a lot, from my own pocket (and anyone who knows the price of a drink on board the TGV will sympathize), and my person (more sympathy, please). Yes, more sympathy, because it was a real war dance. Here I go, I will flatter you and talk to you about your crap book and listen to your confessions about the suffering of your inner child whom you have to console if you want to stop being the ideal prey for manipulators and enpies—

"Enpies?"

"Narcissistic perverts."

"Ah, I see."

. . . and your inner kiddiwink always goes for the most expensive cookies, and I don't dare get out my restaurant coupons, not to look like a dork, and I will pay you compliments, and make you laugh and giggle, and jerk your tears as well (yes, my mom died at Christmas and I went home so I could go and pray at her grave . . . yes, it's sad . . . yes, I put lilies . . . she loved them . . . yes, they wither all too quickly but it's the thought that counts . . . and yes, you are really so stupid but so good, and yes, I am really very stupid but so so good), and I will touch your arm, and tuck a strand of hair behind your ear, and I will seem as if I'm really under your spell, and look I'm even stammering from the emotion, do you realize? But . . . But who's manipulating who here? Hang on a minute, I'm completely entranced . . . Say, will you lend me your book, to help me learn to cope? Go on . . . Go on. If we get married someday, you'll put it in your trousseau, okay? You're so lovely. What's your name? Justine? Like in the Marquis de Sade? No. Nothing. You are beautiful, Justine. Are you coming? Shall we go? No, not to my place, not just yet, to our seats.

And why aren't you coming?

Oh? You have a call to make? To whom? The bridal shop? Ah, no, your boyfriend.

Oh?

Your boyfriend.

Oh, I see. Okay, well then, I'll be off. Will you give me your number anyway, princess? We could . . . we could be friends.

Merde.

I went back to my seat like yesterday at low tide: soaked, dazed, shaken by the waves; my old age under my arm and my tail between my legs.

Shit. She really was a stunner.

And I was in a hell of a mood for a cuddle.

Especially tonight.

I'd just seen my fiancée get married to another guy, for fuck's sake.

My Delacroix pieta was asleep now.

I sat down across from her and observed her against the light.

She reminded me of Lisbeth Salander, the girl with the dragon tattoo.

She was messed up big-time with all her hardware and Goth-Punk regalia, but asleep, she looked like a fragile little girl.

A little sleeping doll. Any enpie's dream.

I tried to retouch her, mentally. Removed her makeup, unstudded her, unpierced her, undyed her, cut her hair, undressed her, redressed her, unneedled her tattoos, and rubbed her hands with cream.

I prepared the stretcher, fixed the canvas, and licked the hairs of my paintbrush before dipping them in the pot.

I was repenting, big-time.

Oh, dearie me . . . What rubbish.

And her slut-face companion still hadn't shown up. Was she telling her boyfriend all about me or what.

Rat-a-tat-tat! Classy Joe, take your revenge!

You know, sweetie, I've just met someone and we really have to talk because my inner little baby-waby is really really afraid of losing her pacifier, now . . .

Or maybe she was telling one of her girlfriends in Nice all about me. Yes I swear! Just like that, in the lounge car. Yes right next to the place where they keep the defibrillator on the wall. Yeah, really, like . . . Yeah, just like I said . . . A really drop-dead gorgeous guy from Paris. Visa Gold card, white shirt, all suntanned. And an orphan on top of it, can you imagine? Hey, like . . . The guy was so hot he was, like, dripping with juice . . . Sounds good, right? Ha ha ha. What? Did I give him my number? Are you crazy or what? Those

Parisians, they're like chickpea socca, you have to eat them with your tips of your fingers . . . Ha ha ha.

Ha ha ha. Lulled by the ebb and flow of my stupidity, I went back to sleep.

4

S ah! Sah! You gotta leave now! You gotta get out dis train. Else you gonna end up at de depot in Garonor, y'know."

A Senegalese infantryman (no, take that back, a Black in a brown uniform with a red cap, a cleaner, but I don't know how to refer to him without making myself look like a little white racist) (a cousin of *lovely Lily who was Somali*) (that's not much more politically correct, either, but it allows me to slip in a reference to a song by Pierre Perret that my mother really liked, and which she passed on to generations of children back in the days when the teacher was always right and you learned everything by heart).

So. I'll start over.

"Sir, sir . . . wake up. We're in Paris."

Man did I feel bad. Did I feel cold. Man, was it dark out there. And man, I was alone on earth in this ghostly compartment.

The sound of vacuum cleaners was piercing my eardrums, I made a face, sighed, pulled on my sandpaper cheeks, shook myself, and was about to leave this cursed place when I noticed a sheet of paper on the shelf by the window.

It was a page torn from a notebook. A drawing. Of me.

Me, smiling in my sleep.

Me thanking Nathan, Patoche, Momo, Arthur, Camille, and all my friends for still being alive.

Still being alive.

And how handsome I was . . . Sorry, the portrait was handsome. So handsome I almost didn't recognize myself.

But yes. It was me. A happy me. A me I hadn't seen in ages. A me that wasn't actually all that old. Or stupid. Or merely a copy. A real me. A nice me. A freehand me. A me who had been liked, a little, but sincerely, in the time it took to sketch me.

And beneath the India ink wash drawing, in very pretty handwriting, very elegant and harmonious, I was captioned, thus:

We live one life, we dream of another, but the one we dream of is our true life.

I don't know why, but I sobered right up just then. A cloak of sadness fell over me. I don't know why. Maybe the sight of my stupid self in the mirror did it.

I took my present and left the train.

5

The platform stretched endlessly before me, night had fallen, I was already homesick, and no one was waiting for me, anywhere.

I walked for a long time into the bleary light of the Gare Montparnasse, patting all my pockets as I hunted for my fucking key-ring.

I thought I'd burst into tears.

The aftereffects, had to be.
Aftereffects. Fatigue.

I still couldn't see anything, these eyes of mine, always losing everything, the eyes of an invalid, my eyes stinging.

I swallowed.

I always swallow.

The famous technique used by divers who have a cold.

6

Are these yours, by any chance?"

All the way at the end of the platform, where it opened out into the station, one of the girls from my compartment had her arm outstretched, my keys jangling in her hand.

Which one?
Take your pick, my friends!

Spirit of Henri, thank you.

ABOUT THE AUTHOR

While working as a high-school French teacher, Anna Gavalda published her first work in 1999, the critically acclaimed collection of short stories *I Wish Someone Were Waiting for Me Somewhere*, which sold over half a million copies in her native France and was published in the US by Penguin in 2003. Gavalda has since published three novels, all of which have become best-sellers across Europe. Her first novel, *Someone I Loved*, was adapted to film in 2009 and her novel *Hunting and Gathering* was made into a film starring Audrey Tautou and Daniel Auteuil. Gavalda's novels and short stories have been translated into over forty languages. She lives in Paris.